8/2022

Cover by Asterielly Designs

The Oddity's Revenge

By S.J. Yanke

For everyone that has ever felt a

little odd

Prologue

Mira Tourmaline was eleven years old when she first started to sprout hairs on her chin. Her mother made her shave every morning to try and hide them, but they only grew back thicker. She was thirteen when her beard and mustache had grown to a length that would put most men to shame, and her family was forced to move from their hometown to a small fishing village.

Her parents were determined to hide her true identity, so they called her Miles and forced her to dress and act like a boy. They lived there in peace for two years, until one day the boy who had become best friend was too rough during an innocent scuffle, he tore her shirt open and her secret was revealed. The boy was terrified of her and yelled out that she had been cursed.

The townsfolk gathered around to see what the boy had been yelling about, when they saw Mira's chest, they dragged her to her home and demanded that her and her parents leave. They chased them and threw rocks at them until they were on the outskirts of town, telling them they would be hanged if they tried to come back.

They walked until they reached a port far enough away that their story couldn't reach them, and took up residence in a small hut just outside of town. Mira's mother blamed her for all of their unfortunate luck and beat her unconscious when her father was out looking for a job on the docks. She awoke sometime later, to see a man talking with her mother, she watched as the man handed her mother a fist full of money, and her mother walked away. Her vision blurred again and she fell back into unconsciousness.

When she woke again she was swaying gently, she opened her eyes and saw that she was lying in a hammock inside of a small wooden room. She got unsteadily to her feet, took a deep breath and stepped out into a small passageway.

She made her way up a tight staircase and onto the deck of a ship. She had never been on a ship before and was awestruck at the size of it and the men around her that were as rough as the wind beaten sails above her. They stopped and stared at her as she walked past, some spit at her feet.

The captain of the ship was at the wheel; he spotted her and waved her over to him. When she reached him, he wouldn't look her in the eye but said:

"I am Captain Ross, this is the Sea's Glory. Your mother sold you into my servitude for five years, she also told me about your... condition. If you earn your keep, and prove worthy, you may be commissioned onto my ship as a true sailor at the end of your indenture. If not, I will dump you at the nearest port and leave you there." He turned his eyes toward her, giving her a sweeping glance. "You can start by scrubbing the deck." With that she was dismissed.

The years went by swiftly and she quickly learned the ropes, earning praise from Captain Ross. He turned out to be a kind and caring man and she silently thanked her mother for selling her to him and not someone cruel that would no doubt abuse her further. He kept her secret and made her feel safe for the first time in her life.

When she turned twenty and her servitude was over, the captain called her to his quarters, he was thoroughly impressed with her dedication to the ship and had another offer for her. He had become sick and needed to return to land for treatment. He promoted Mira to first mate and asked her to take over his shipping routes while he healed. She agreed to temporarily take his place, but worried about what the crew would think of his decision.

As she expected, they did not take it well, they beat her until they thought she was unconscious and began to form a plan, Thomas, Captain Ross's original first mate, told the rest of the crew that they should wait it out and that the Captain would come to his senses and give the ship over to him instead.

However, just one month after he became bed ridden, Captain Ross died, leaving the ship and its routes to Mira. The crew became so enraged that they ambushed her outside of a tavern on her way to the ship, telling her they planned to take the ship as their own.

In the middle of the scuffle, Mira's shirt was torn open and her secret was once again revealed. The crew was enraged at her and the captain's deceit. They beat her bloody and dragged her to the ship and threw her into the ocean.

She swam back toward the ship and was clinging to the side when she heard the men, they were terrified of her, saying that she was cursed and the ship was now too. They were determined not to set it on fire and be done with the whole affair. She quickly climbed a rope ladder and stood on the railing, she screamed at them to leave, damning them all and telling them she would curse anyone who came near her or her ship. As they all fled, she dropped to the deck and wept for all of her misfortune.

When the sun rose the next morning, many of the crew was on the dock near the ship, planning to set the ship on fire so Mira and her curse would be done with. However, they all gaped at what they saw. Mira was standing at the ship's wheel. She was dressed in a lady's gown, cut short in the front so she could move easier, and wore men's breeches and boots underneath. She had traded her sailor cap for a silk top hat with a pair of goggles resting on the brim.

She swore from that day forward, she would no longer hide. She would wear her beard proudly and save anyone else who was labeled a freak. She could no longer bare the thought of someone being mistreated for something as simple as the way their body was presented.

She grinned wildly as she turned the ship out to sea, waving at the crowd on the dock. The last thing they saw was the new name she had scrawled on the back of the ship: The Oddity's Revenge.

One

Twelve Years Later

"You think you can join my crew just because you have a talking bird?" Mira's gems all snickered behind her.

The captain of The Oddity's Revenge and her crew were walking through the town market in some god-awful port that smelled too strongly of the slop buckets that were tossed out of back windows. They had only been in port for an hour and the street rats were already following them.

"Let's hear her out, Cap," Topaz said, looking back at the child that was trying her best to keep up with them. "All of us are more than meets the eye, why can't she be?"

Topaz was her first mate, she

found him chained to a wall in a tavern when he was nineteen years old. He was being forced to charm his pet snake, a python they later named Amethyst, for his dinner, while the innkeeper collected the coins that were being tossed his way. He was thin as a reed and could barely lift the snake, but his muddy green eyes had caught her attention, and held it. When he smiled at her she noticed that his teeth had all been filed to a point. She thought that the tavern owner must have done this to make him look more like his snake and she knew she wouldn't be leaving port without him. She asked him what his name was but he couldn't recall what it was, so she called him Topaz to compliment her own gemstone name.

He now had rolling muscles and a chiseled frame from long years working at sea, and could lift the now eight-foot long snake with one hand. He had grown out his black hair so that it fell about his shoulders and had an impressive mustache that he tended to curl around a finger when he was thinking.

"She might have some tricks up her sleeve," Mira replied, "but I don't want a bird, or a child squawking all over my ship. I have a hard enough time babysitting you lot." Mira kept a swift pace, trying to deter the young girl from following. She couldn't have been older than nine, smelled as if she hadn't bathed for at least four of those years. Her brown hair was so matted that it gave Mira's own filthy locks a run for their money. Her skin was filthy and it was hard to tell its original color. Mira could already imagine the fleas that would attack her ship if she let this girl aboard, but still, she did remind Mira a bit of herself when she was that age. Atop the girl's shoulder was the most obnoxiously colored bird Mira had ever seen, it was constantly squawking, "Dar she blows! Abandon ship!" She could already see herself squeezing the life out of it and tossing it overboard.

She was about to turn and scare her off for good, when the girl suddenly cut in front of her, and she was forced to stop. She held her chin high and cleared her throat. Mira gave an amused huff and gestured for the girl to speak.

"I know you don't allow just anyone on your ship Miss, that's why I've been practicing." The girl said with a stubborn lift to her chin.

"Practicing what, child? Your

letters?" Mira laughed and looked over her shoulder at her crew, when she turned back the girl was looking at her through a very familiar spyglass. Her hand went swiftly to her belt where it was indeed missing. She snatched the girl's hand and pressed a blade to her pinky.

"Well then, a thief is it? Tell me why I shouldn't feed your little finger to our dear Amethyst." She tossed her head back to indicate the python that circled around Topaz's neck and arm, on cue, the snake stuck her long tongue out to smell the child.

Mira was thoroughly impressed, and had to admit that the girl had a skill she needed. If the girl could steal from her, she could easily pick the pockets of anyone Mira needed information from. She glanced back at her crew to see that they had all drawn their own blades and were standing at her back, ready to handle the girl for her. All except Tope that is. He stood to the side, a smile playing at his lips and one brow raised. Mira rolled her eyes at him and he gave her a small shrug. She tightened her grip on the girl's wrist and she dropped the spyglass with a whimper.

"What's your name then, little

thief?" Mira demanded, her face inches from the girl's.

"S-s-sasha, Miss." She stammered.

"Well then, S-s-sasha, what's your favorite gem?" Mira smiled and dropped the girl's hand; the crew behind her gave a small cheer and clapped the girl on the back. Mira turned to continue onto the tavern she was originally headed to.

"My favorite gem, Miss?" Sasha asked, confusion in her voice.

"Well you can't go by Sasha if you plan on being a part of my crew, and I'm not saying you are yet," she warned. "We'll need to put those quick hands of yours to the test first."

The girl's eyes lit up and she gave a loud whoop of excitement.

"Thank you Miss! Oh thank you, thank you!" She clung to Mira's hand and jumped up and down.

"Leave off, you." She chuckled as she tugged her arm free of the girl's grip.

"I've always been fond of them big green stones all of the grannies wear," Sasha said looking thoughtful.

"Big green stones, eh? Those would be emeralds, I'm sure," Mira replied.

She was thinking of another way to

test the girl's skills when they had arrived at the tavern and she stood back to read the advert posted in the window.

ONCE IN A LIFETIME SHOW

Beneath the words was a crude drawing of a woman's dress front. This wouldn't have been out of the ordinary, except this advert showed three bumps beneath the fabric, not two.

"This looks to be the place, Cap" said Spinel in a low voice.

Spinel was easily the roughest member of the Oddity's Revenge; she was just over five feet, with a cloud of golden curls. Her heart shaped mouth was worn in a permanent scowl, her nose wrinkled as if she smelled something foul. She walked as if she had just stepped off of a horse and wore men's boots under her long skirt.

Men would often stare after her but quickly avert their eyes if she turned her gaze their way, but she was used to the stares. If they weren't staring at the scar that ran from her brow to chin, they were staring at the fact that her right arm was metal. She had lost it and gained her scar when she was six years old. Her father's fishing raft had run aground during a storm, and she had been flung from the small vessel onto a rocky island, only to be pinned between the raft and the rocks. Her father had to pull her free and swam them both back to shore in a desperate attempt to save her life.

She was also the only member of the crew that had come from a decent background, her family was poor and she went without her arm until she was seventeen and joined Mira's crew. Her parents had taken her to a circus two years after her accident and she had fallen in love with the lion performance, there was a male and a female and they were the most beautiful things she had ever seen. After the show, she snuck backstage to see them up close. To her amazement they weren't in a cage, instead they lay in an open crate, snuggling two cubs. She opened a crate that read "Lion Chow" near the entrance and found that it was an ice chest with bloody steaks inside, she took two out and approached the crate slowly. She threw the steaks to opposite sides of the crate and waited until the adult lions were busy eating before slowly reaching in and grabbing a cub, stuffing it into her sack and locking the crate. She ran as fast as she could through the crowds to her waiting parents, not turning back when she heard shouts from the lion tamer. Her parents didn't notice the cub until they were halfway to their village, when they looked back to see Spinel and the cub curled around each other sound asleep.

"It would appear so." Mira replied to Spinel.

"Tell me, *Emerald*," she said, turning to the small girl, and gesturing to the sign. "You've stolen a mere spyglass, but have you ever stolen a person?"

Later that evening, Mira traded her dress and corset for rich leather pants, a man's silk shirt and finely tailored jacket. She took the golden hoops out of her ears, in exchange for a single diamond stud. She left her treasured top hat on her desk, and let her locks fall free from their leather band. She then took a clean rag and washed the worst of the grime from her honey-colored face. As a final touch, she took out a razor and cleaned up the hairs under her chin, then rubbed sweet oil through her mustache to make it curl at the ends.

It was much easier to steal in foreign ports when she dressed as a rich man, than if she went about dressed as herself. Female captains tend to stand out, but *bearded* female captains were unforgettable. They would be on to her scheme in a heartbeat.

When she was ready, she met Tope on the deck and together, they began the short journey back to the tavern. He was equally disguised and she took a moment to admire the hug of his breeches as he turned to march down the dock.

"Are you sure she is the real deal?" She asked as they made their way through the muck-infested streets, dodging beggars and pickpockets. She had no reason to doubt him, he had never let her down before, but the idea of a three-breasted lady was a far fetched one.

"She's all we've heard about for the last three ports, I doubt she would raise that much attention if she was a fraud. Besides, I've heard just as much about her devil of a father and how he treats her," he said darkly. "I overheard some men this morning saying they wouldn't be going back tonight because they don't like their goods to be damaged."

Mira didn't like this added

information, she was already upset about having to smuggle someone out of a frequently visited establishment, hearing just how poorly she was being treated darkened her mood further. They were approaching the tavern so she made her best attempt at looking bored. They knocked on the door and waited until a portly man answered, Mira noticed that one of his eyes was swollen and had a yellow bruise under it.

"What's this about? Pirates ain't allowed in my establishment, they tend to take more than they give," he said, sniffing and giving them each an interested once-over. "Tend to forget their manners on the boat too."

Mira and Tope turned to look over each other, they thought they had done a fine job of hiding the fact that they were pirates, apparently they hadn't.

"We've come for the show of a lifetime." Topaz said mockingly, "That is, if your… establishment can provide it. It doesn't seem like the type of place a hidden gem would be found." He gave the man and his store a disgusted look, "Come along Captain, I'm sure we can find a more entertaining evening elsewhere." Tope swung a heavy coin purse around his finger as they turned to leave. She caught a glance of the man's face and had to use a cough to cover her laugh, he had turned an alarming shade of blue.

"Wait, damn you!" His eyes were greedy as he eyed Tope's coin purse. "You'll find no better entertainment in this town! Maybe even the entire world! Did I hear you call that fellow Captain? You'll be from the cruise ship then? I would say we've had our fair share of sailors, but no captains yet. None so fine as yourself to be sure! Your first drink is on the house sir. And I would warn you against any mistreatment to my establishment, I'm not one to be crossed." He puffed out his chest as he said this, but the only effect it had was to make his potbelly even more pronounced.

They shared a look and turned back. The poor man was wringing his hands together and bouncing from foot to foot, waiting for an answer.

"A bottle of your finest liquor, and the Captain here gets thirty private minutes with the star," Tope said, he had crossed his large arms across his thick chest and taken a wide stance, showing off his muscular thighs. She would have loved to be standing across from him, as to better enjoy the view, but now wasn't the time.

The man continued to fidget while he thought this over. Mira shrugged her shoulders and turned once more to leave.

"Wait!" the man shouted again, "You have a deal. But if any harm should come to the girl, I'll have both of your heads above my mantel." He said as he turned to lead them inside.

"Oh trust me sir, your daughter will be in the best hands she's ever known." Tope said as he tossed the man a coin.

"My-but- how did you-" he started, but Mira cut him off with a wave of her hand.

"Bring me to her," she said, deepening her voice to impersonate a man.

"Of course, right away. If you'll follow me, I'll take you to her room." The man shuffled forward, taking a ring of keys from his belt.

"I have started to lock her in her room before the performances, the men that come here have been demanding more and more from her. It is for her safety, I assure you." Mira had other ideas as to why he locked her in, but she kept them to herself. He continued to ramble on as they climbed a narrow staircase to the second floor. Mira made note of the nail marks and what looked like boot prints carved into the walls. At the top of the stairs was a door with two large locks on the outside, the man cleared his throat and seemed embarrassed by them. He quickly unlocked them and swung the door open to revealed yet another set of stairs, this one even more cramped and steep than the last.

She raised an eyebrow at the man and made to push past him, but he blocked her way with his meaty arm.

"Thirty minutes, Captain. If I find that my Elizabeth has been harmed in anyway, I will shoot you down and mount your head. You have my word," he threatened.

Mira gave a deep chuckle, "As you've promised before sir, trust me, your daughter is in very good hands." She flashed him a toothy grin and slammed the door closed behind her, then made her way to the top of the stairs.

Whatever she had been expecting, it wasn't this. White silk hung from the walls and the posters of a large and overstuffed bed. There were gas lamps in every corner and a large dressing table covered in creams and perfumes in every variety. On one wall stood the largest wardrobe Mira had ever seen, it hung open to display gowns and coats in every color under the sun. On another wall was a long table stacked high with teas, cakes, sweets, and wines. A small figure sat with her back to the door, adjusting pins in her light brown hair. From what Mira could see, she had soft curves and long elegant fingers, her shoulders drooped and she had an uneasy air about her. It intrigued Mira.

"Father, I told you I wouldn't be ready for another fifteen minutes. I thought we agreed that I would have a say in when I am to give my performances now?" Elizabeth said.

After not receiving an answer, she whipped around, ready to attack her father but stopped short when she saw Mira standing there. Mira was shocked by what she saw; she was looking at quite possibly the most beautiful person she had ever seen. The woman had large full brows, serious deep brown eyes and a very full mouth. Mira swallowed deeply and tried not to let her emotions show on her face.

"Who are you and what do you think you're doing in my room, sir? How did you get past the locks?" She stopped herself short and paled. "My father let you in, didn't he?" she whispered.

She brought a hand to her mouth and tears filled her eyes, "Please," she started, "Please, just leave. I don't know what he has promised you, but I can't, I can't give you anything. No, please no." She began to cry in earnest as Mira took off her jacket and started to undo the buttons on her shirt.

"Please! No! I'll give you my coin purse. I will tell my father that we went through with what you want from me. Just please don't touch me!"

She stopped short and stared open mouthed as Mira ripped her shirt open to expose her chest.

"Calm down, woman! You'll have the entire place down on our heads if you don't hush." Mira growled.

Elizabeth slowly turned her head to the side and furrowed her brow. "I've never been asked to entertain a woman before." She raked her eyes over Mira's figure, raising an eyebrow in interest. "Why wouldn't you just take the beard off?" she asked.

"It's attached, my dear," Mira explained, her voice back to its natural velvety smooth lilt. "And I didn't come for entertainment. I came to make you an offer; I am Mira Tourmaline, captain of The Oddity's Revenge. Have you heard of my crew and I?" She asked as she started to do the buttons up on her shirt.

Elizabeth nodded slowly, her brows knitted together. Then her eyes grew wide as she realized what that meant. She was being saved.

"You're here because you've heard of what he makes me do? You know what he allows those disgusting men do to me?" Her voice quivered as she became angry. "Tell me you're here to take me away."

Mira nodded her head, "If you agree to come with me, you also agree to follow my rules. You agree to respect my ship and my crew. You don't have to do what you do here," she gestured to what Elizabeth was wearing, which wasn't much. "But you will earn your keep, everyone on the crew does, on the sea and in port. We've all come from difficult places, we're all looking for some chance at freedom. This can be yours, if you agree to my terms."

She crossed her arms as she finished and continued to look around the room. Elizabeth stood and began gathering bottles and tins from her dressing table.

"I will do my best Captain, I know nothing of sailing but I will learn. I will figure out a way to earn your trust and my place." She rambled on as she tried in vain to stuff two very large dresses into her small trunk. Mira crossed the room with quick steps and grabbed Elizabeth's wrist.

"First rule, none of this is coming." Mira said as she gestured around the room, "You will leave your old life behind. All of it." She paused here and gave her wardrobe a meaningful look. She let go and stepped back, crossing her arms once more.

"But- these are my things. My father said I earned every scrap of lace in this room. I've worked hard for my things." Elizabeth stuck her chin in the air and pouted, it made her look like a child and made Mira wonder how old she was.

"These are my rules girl, once you leave this place, you won't be returning. We can't run the risk of someone recognizing you or drawing attention to ourselves when we leave. We have to make it look like you were kidnapped, not that you left willingly." Mira started to pace, they were running out of time. Elizabeth looked around the lush room for a long moment.

"Are you coming or not?" Mira demanded, becoming uneasy. "We don't have much time before your father comes to collect me."

Elizabeth had started to chew her lower lip. Now that she was closer, Mira could see what the men Tope overheard had meant when they called her "damaged goods". She had finger marks on her upper arms, her nails had been bitten short and she could see the edge of a bruise peaking out form under her hairline. She had large bags under her eyes that she had tried in vain to cover with makeup.

"Is your father the one that beats you? Or does he allow the men to do that too?" Mira asked quietly.

Elizabeth sat heavily on her bed and buried her face in her hands, beginning to cry once more. Mira stayed where she was and waited until Elizabeth was ready.

"It hasn't always been this way,"

she started. "It began when I was twelve. He made me show men my breasts as they grew. When I was fifteen he made me dance for them, taking off more clothes if they gave him more coin." They were both silent for a moment.

"Soon the men got bored of the dancing, they would throw their drinks at me and demand that I smile more, enjoy myself, they didn't like knowing that I didn't want to be there. Then one day a man came and offered my father a great sum of money if he would allow the man to bed me." She paused again, blowing her nose and wiping under her eyes. "My father is a greedy man. He cares about money above all else, even me." She looked up at Mira, defiance in her dark amber eyes.

"What about your mother?" Mira asked.

"She died giving birth to me, sometimes I wish I would have gone with her." She replied quietly.

Mira approached her slowly and held out a hand.

"If you choose to join us, we will take care of you, I will take care of you. You'll never have to do anything you don't wish to ever again," she told her.

Elizabeth hesitated for a breath, than reached out and clutched Mira's hand. When they touched, Mira felt a surge of heat flare in her chest; she blinked in surprise then schooled her features.

·   "Make sure you grab a few things of value, I'll wait for you at the door." Mira kissed the delicate hand and turned to go, taking the steps slowly just in case the girl's father was waiting close by. She put an ear to the door and waited for Elizabeth, she could hear her gathering more than a few things and rolled her eyes. She knew that life on a ship would be an adjustment for her; she just hoped she wouldn't make everyone's too difficult while she found her bearings. It grew quiet upstairs and Mira was about to see what was taking so long when a loud thump sounded from the other side of the door.

"Shit," she mumbled, checking her pocket watch, "Out of time."

Elizabeth appeared beside her, nearly out of breath. She was wearing a ridiculous hat and had a rather large looking bag under her arm. Mira arched a brow at her, she flashed an apologetic smile and said, "That will be my father. If he is anything, he's punctual."

Mira rested a hand on the dagger at her waist and looked back at the door. Elizabeth tucked a few stray hairs under her hat and nodded at Mira to open the door. She did so slowly and was met by the sight of Elizabeth's father laying face down on the floor, he groaned quietly and held a hand to the back of his head.

"Quickly now," Topaz hissed, coming out of the shadows. He too had a hand on his dagger and was looking over his shoulder to the bottom of the stairs. They could hear men's shouts and laughter coming from deeper in the store and Mira guessed that they had come for a chance to see Elizabeth.

Mira pushed Elizabeth into Tope's outstretched hand and bent to tie her father's hands behind his back, shoving him inside the door that led to Elizabeth's room. She closed it on him and turned to the others.

"He'll be up soon, move!" She whispered loudly.

Topaz turned to them and gave Elizabeth a sweeping gaze.

"Whoa, I've never seen a... hat that big before" He said, clearly looking at her chest.

"Oh Jesus, not now Tope," Mira said with an eye roll, "This whole plan will come down on our heads if we don't get out of here!" She gave them a shove and rushed down the stairs.

They slowed as they reached the bottom. Mira drew her pistol and held it to her lips in a gesture to make sure her companions stayed quiet. She poked her head around the wall to make sure their way was clear. Seeing that it was, she waved the others to move ahead of her while she watched the hall beyond. She was just about to follow them when a door at the end of the hall opened and a very drunk man stumbled out, she glanced over her shoulder and found that Tope and Elizabeth had hidden somewhere near the front door. She holstered her gun and stumbled off of the steps.

"Where the hell can a man take a piss in this place?" she asked, doing her best to sound as drunk as the man in front of her looked. "I've gone around in circles! I'm about to use that rather nasty looking house plant if I can't find the back door!" she sauntered closer to the man and he began to chuckle.

"Your first time here, eh?" he

asked, "I was headed that way myself, come, I'll show you where it is."

As soon as the man turned his back, Mira struck him over the back of the head with the hilt of her dagger and caught him before he hit the ground. She led him over to a chair and propped him up to make it look like he had simply fallen asleep. She rushed back to the front of the store when there came a muffled yell from above her.

"*Shit,*" she mumbled again, tonight was not going as smoothly as she would have liked.

She ran to catch up with the others when Elizabeth's father appeared at the top of the steps, his face was bright red and he was breathing as if he had just run a mile.

"Where is she?" he demanded, stumbling down the steps as fast as his stubby legs could take him. "Stop! Stop him!" He cried.

The door at the end of the hall crashed open and a string of men came rushing out.

"Shit," Mira cursed again, this was really going to ruin her night.

She turned toward the front door to find it standing open, "Good man Tope," she mumbled, running forward. The men behind her started shouting and some had drawn their weapons.

"What's going on here?" The man in front bellowed, looking from Mira to Elizabeth's father.

"That man has taken Elizabeth! Stop him!" He cried, clutching his chest and panting more deeply now.

The men charged after her, yelling profanities and accusing Elizabeth's father of lying so the girl wouldn't have to perform tonight. Mira thought quickly, making a rash decision. She stopped in the doorway and turned back to the group, turning back and aiming her pistol at the gas lamps that was hung from the low ceiling. She fired twice and the lights went out, sparks rained down on the men, earning her a curse as more than one body fell. She wrenched the door closed and forced two large barrels that were close by in front of it. Then turned and took off in the direction of the docks. She heard footsteps behind her and glanced back to see Tope carrying Elizabeth's bag, and Elizabeth clutching her hat, a wild grin on her face.

"That was wonderful!" she shouted, "Did you see my fathers face?"

Her eyes were wild and she was practically dancing with glee.

"We will see it and more if you don't hurry up!" Tope yelled to her.

Elizabeth clamped her hand down harder onto her hat and picked up her pace, from a snail's pace to a turtle's giant. It was clear that her skirts were weighing her down, but Mira wasn't convinced that she would be much faster without them.

"This way!" Mira called as she headed down a darkened alley.

They ducked behind more barrels as the men from the storefront ran by, followed slowly by Elizabeth's father. He was shouting at them to send for a sheriff to the cruise ship that was in port and to not let them get away. Elizabeth giggled behind her hand and looked over at Mira.

"A cruise ship? But I thought yours was old and wooden?" She whispered.

"Old?" Mira balked, and Tope chuckled, "The Oddity isn't *old,* she has been around for a few years, but I wouldn't call her old," Mira continued, clearly offended.

"I would," Tope said, "She's a big old beast, smells like one too, if I'm being honest."

Mira turned on him, her dagger

out. "Just for that, you can scrub her deck when we get back, top to bottom, until we reach the next port."

Tope openly gaped, "What!" He yelled, and she slapped a hand over his mouth.

"Get comfortable, they'll be keeping an eye on the ships for the rest of the night, try to rest, I'll take the watch," she told them, turning away and mumbling to herself about the state of her ship.

"Sleep here?" Elizabeth asked looking around with a disgusted look on her face. "But it's filthy," she whined.

Tope laughed quietly again, then leaned close to whisper: "Get used to filth, Miss, The Oddity isn't very clean either."

Mira threw her dagger without turning; it stuck into the wall next to his head. Elizabeth jumped back with a yelp and Tope chuckled, snatching it out of the wall and tossing it back to Mira.

"Come here, Love, I'll keep you warm." He said, pulling Elizabeth to his chest.

Mira let out a low growl that made Elizabeth stiffen.

"What?" Tope said, "We can't have her freezing to death her first night with us, can we?"

Mira's reply was muffled as she sank lower into her own coat. Tope pulled Elizabeth closer and pushed her head onto his chest, she watched her breath play with the hair poking out of his shirt as she fell asleep.

Two

The next morning, the trio decided that it would draw less attention if they made their way back to the docks separately. Topaz was off gathering a small list of supplies while Mira trailed behind Elizabeth, making sure that she was nearby if she needed her help.

She had made the girl change from her lace gown into rough sailing clothes to make her less recognizable. They had passed several groups of men searching for her and so far the disguise was working, they only had a little further before they reached the safety of the docks.

She was thinking of the way Elizabeth's hips swayed beneath her breeches when a shout rang out. She shot forward through the crowded street, looking around for Elizabeth, but couldn't see her anywhere. How could she have gotten out of her sight so quickly? She really needed to sort out what was happening in her mind.

She heard a muffled cry and a few women shouting to her right and headed toward them. Down a small side street, a few men were huddled in a circle and two women were hurrying away, clearly not wanting to be around the men and what they were doing.

Mira surged forward, grabbing one of the men by the shoulder and shoving him backwards. Before her lay an unconscious Elizabeth, the men around her were arguing as to who would retrieve her father and how they would split the reward for her return.

Mira counted the men off; there were four of them. She sighed in discontent, she had fought multiple men off before, but this was less than ideal. She sent up a silent prayer, hoping Topaz would somehow appear soon, and took a deep breath.

She took out the man next to her quickly, swinging her elbow hard into his hose and kicking out his legs. She crouched down as the man on her other side swung at her, she brought the heel of her hand up and into his throat as she rose. The one across from her was standing with his mouth hanging open, staring in shock as she turned to him. She took two long strides and punched him square in the eye, knocking him unconscious.

The last man had taken a few steps back and had watched this play out with an amused smile.

"You must be the man that took her, I must admit I'm impressed. We've been thinking of a way to smuggle her out of that hell house for years now. I would have taken her home for myself if these mongrels hadn't been with me. How about we share her? A week at yours, a week at mine?" The man said all of this while slowly circling Mira; she was determined to keep herself between the man and Elizabeth.

Instead of answering him, she took out her longest blade, stopping him in his tracks. He raised a brow at her.

"She's that good, eh? Alright then, let's have at it." He took out his own blade and rolled his shoulders, giving her a "come here" gesture with his hand. He raised a brow at her when she didn't move, then let out a low chuckle and ran at her. Mira stayed where she was, and kicked him hard in the groin when he got close enough, he howled in pain and fell to the side. She brought her knee up into his nose and it gave a satisfying crunch. She stood up and rolled her neck.

"I am getting too old to fight this many men on my own," she mumbled to herself. "Two I can handle, but four? Four is getting to be too much."

She was in the process of dragging the second man behind a bush when Tope appeared, smiling and whistling, a bag slung over his shoulder.

He raised a brow at her as he looked around at the rest of the men lying in the street.

"Having a party are we?" He asked, amusement dancing in his eyes.

"Shut up and help me." Mira growled at him.

Mira heard Elizabeth groan as they stepped onto the dock. She was slung over Topaz's shoulder, and gave another small groan as she reached up to feel a lump on the side of her head.

"You're awake," Mira said quietly, "Keep still, we're nearly there. You were knocked out by a group of men trying to collect the bounty your father put out for you."

"I'm going to puke," Elizabeth groaned in response.

"Off you go then, I don't want you to get sick on my good shirt," Topaz said, practically dropping her to the deck.

Elizabeth crawled to the side of the dock and promptly threw up into the sea, Mira stooped to rub small circles on her back. When she was done, she sat up and Topaz shoved a handkerchief in her direction.

"Come now, we're only a short distance away," Mira pointed down the dock to an enormous pirate ship.

Its sails were gray and weather beaten; some of the boards on the side were rotting and it needed a fresh coat of paint. Below deck wasn't much better, the crew's cabins were growing damp as the boards rotted. You basically had to swim for your dinner in the galley and some stray barnacles had made a home in the cupboards,

Mira glanced over in time to see Elizabeth grimace at the sight of it, she knew the ship was in dire need of repairs but they hadn't been able to stay in one port long enough to have the repairs done. Still, she was proud of her ship and turned an eyebrow up at Elizabeth, daring her to speak ill of it.

To her surprise, Elizabeth's look of uncertainty had turned to one of awe as they approached. She saw her taking in the lanterns strung from one end to the other, the carved designs that Spinel had etched into every surface she could, and the beautiful figurehead at its front, a woman whose long hair covered her naked breasts, she was cradling an enormous piece of obsidian in front of her chest. Mira had looked high and low for a piece large enough to fit in the woman's large hands.

She couldn't help but smile. She was very proud of her ship, and all they had done together.

"I know she isn't much to look at," Mira said, "But she's our home and our safe haven, I hope she will be yours too."

Elizabeth smiled and Mira noticed tears in the corners of her eyes.

"By the way," Mira said, "what's your favorite gem?"

"Zircon," Elizabeth replied, not

missing a beat. She turned and smiled at Mira, excitement dancing in her eyes.

Mira stepped onto the gangway and held out her hand. "Zircon is it than, welcome to The Oddity's Revenge.

Three

Mira came above deck, looking over another map as she headed toward the helm she didn't need to look up as she weaved her way around various objects and people, she knew her ship better than she knew herself. As she approached the three short steps that led to the aft of the ship, she stopped, could just hear the sound of a scrub brush that meant Zircon was there scrubbing the deck, she was about to turn around when she heard her speak.

"Why does she make everyone pick new names?" Mira ducked her head as she heard this, knowing the Zircon meant her. She peaked up over the edge of the helm to get a better look.

"It's like a snake shedding its skin," she heard Peridot reply, "We leave our old lives behind when we join The Oddity's Revenge. Choosing a new name is just one of the many ways we do that, it holds the most significance, I think." Mira smiled at that, picking a new name was her favorite part of getting a new crewmember.

"Why gems though?" Zircon asked, scrubbing at a particularly nasty piece of bird poop.

"Do you know the captain's last name?" Peridot asked still not looking up. She stuck her tongue out a bit as she drew a line, mapping their way to their next destination. Mira laughed at the sight of it.

"I thought she was just called Captain Mira, I've never heard her called anything else." Zircon replied, sitting up on her knees and wiping sweat from her brow.

Peridot let out a huff of laughter at the same time Mira did, "Were you always called 'Elizabeth, the three breasted lady'?" She said, arching an eyebrow at the younger woman.

"No, I suppose not," Zircon mumbled, her cheeks turning an adorable shade of pink.

"It's Tourmaline," Peridot said, turning back to her maps, "Like the gem that is used as a shield against unwanted energies. Quite fitting if you think about it." Mira smiled again, she always appreciated the way Peridot could romanticize things. But she had to admit that her given name did fit her and her cause very well.

"What about this ship? How does a person like Mira become captain of a ship?" she heard Zircon ask.

Mira didn't like the sound of the question or where this conversation was going. She didn't like to speak of her troubled childhood, and she certainly didn't like to hear other people discussing what her mother had done to her even more. She left the telling of her story to Peridot, everyone on the ship heard it when they officially joined her crew, but she didn't want to be in earshot when she did it.

She cleared her throat and stomped her feet to make it sound as if she was approaching, than walked up the steps, eyes on her map.

"Can you have a look at this Per?" Mira asked, than stopped short when she saw Zircon. She was still on her knees, scrubbing brush in hand, her hair was wind swept and her face was now beat red from working in the sun. Mira's own face turned red as her eyes roamed lower and noticed that Zircon's dress was sopping wet and was slipping lower due to the added weight of the water. She quickly looked at a spot over her shoulder and cleared her throat.

"Give us a moment, would you Zircon?" She said, clearly uncomfortable.

"Of course, Captain," Zircon mumbled as she gathered her scrub brush and bucket, moving to the opposite end of the boat.

"Well that was awkward," Peridot laughed as she watched Mira watching Zircon walk away.

Mira snapped her head back to Peridot and cleared her throat again, "I don't know what you mean," she said, clearly knowing what she meant.

"You know, there are some couples that take on extra partners. It would be quite scandalous, but would that be anything new on this ship? We could make an act out of it," Peridot said, her eyes alight with mischief.

"I think being a bearded female captain is enough scandal for me, thank you very much," she replied, snapping the map back open and put it in front of the other woman's face.

"I have our next port," she said.

The port she had chosen was one of their favorites. The entire village usually made its way to the ship one night or another, always welcoming the crew and Mira like old friends. Still, Mira was worried about being ambushed by more men sent by Zircon's father, so she sent Emerald out as soon as they were tied off. She saw her come back in only twenty minutes, bringing with her a wanted poster. The poster advertised a reward of $10,000 for the return of Miss Elizabeth Creed, a sum that Elizabeth -Zircon- had laughed at, saying her father would never give that amount up.

Mira and Topaz set out to their favorite tavern just after sunset, both disguised as merchants as they hung up flyers saying that the crew would be ready to perform the next day.

SHIP OF WONDERS!
BEARDED LADY
SNAKE CHARMER
FORTUNE TELLER
LION TAMER
FLYING TWINS BIRD GIRL

The flyer wasn't anything special, but the townsfolk gathered around them as soon as they were hung. Everyone tended to stare at the crew when they walked through markets, even the ones that they had been to before. Mira had to admit that they stood out more than the average sailors.

The most eye catching members were the Quartz Twins, Aventurine and Citrine, they were both well over six feet tall with skin and hair as white as freshly fallen snow. They wore smoked glasses at all times to protect their light blue eyes from the sun's rays. People who had never seen them before couldn't tell them apart, for even though they were brother and sister, they both had waist length wavy hair, beautiful full lips, and long muscular limbs. They wore matching brown leather vests, breeches and soft leather slippers.

The one sure give away to tell them apart was the scar on the back of Aventurine's left arm, she got it during one of their first performances when her brother had dropped her thirty feet onto the deck below and the bone went through her skin. She wore it with pride, but never let her brother forget his mistake. They had discovered their love for trapezing when they were small and had to run away from the other children in their village, they would often wind up in trees or roofs, hiding from the stones and horrible words that were thrown at them.

When Mira and Topaz arrived at the tavern, they separated at the door and made their way around the room on separate walls. They trained their ears to catch any hint of an ambush or talk of Mira or Zircon but only heard the usual gossip of a small town.

When they reached the bar they sat next to each other and ordered their drinks, the barkeep nodded at Mira in acknowledgement. His name was Samuel and he was one of the only friends Mira had made outside of her crew, he was known for his ability to keep secrets and always having interesting bits of information for Mira. He was a tall older gentleman with white hair and a large handlebar mustache; he usually gave Topaz a bit of grief about not being able to grow one as impressive as his.

He slowly made his way to the opposite end of the bar near a large group of men, then made his way back to them.

"Cap," he said. He had been cleaning a mug with a dirty rag and set it down on the bar, looking over Mira and Topaz. "Heard about that performer girl that went missing a few ports over?"

Mira was in the process of taking a drink of her ale but her hand froze in midair. This was Samuel's way of telling her that trouble was near and that she needed to watch her back. She looked at the group of men at the other end of the bar from the corner of her eye, and took a long drink.

"Damn shame," Topaz told Samuel.

"That it is," Samuel nodded his agreement. "If I was Miss Tourmaline, I would keep a low profile for a while, stick to the sea. There's more than one posse out looking for that girl to collect the reward," he gave Mira a pointed look.

"Well you know that old crone," Topaz said. He took a drink of his ale and looked at Mira. "Never knows when to quit or when something is a bad idea."

Topaz and Samuel stared Mira down as she finished her ale, slammed the mug down onto the bar and let out a loud and unladylike burp. She was becoming nervous and needed to get back to the ship.

"Pay the man, Tope," she said as she wiped her mouth on the back of her sleeve. "Have you heard, Sam? That bearded woman and her freaks are in town." Samuel's eyes flared when Mira said "freaks."

"I bet you could get a discount on your ticket if you offered them a keg of this piss water," she said before she turned on her heel and headed for the door quicker than she would have liked. She could feel the heat creeping up her neck as the other patrons in the tavern looked after her and hoped that Topaz was close behind her, she wasn't sure she would be able to fight anyone off if they came after her.

The next evening before the customers came aboard, Mira took Emerald and Zircon around the ship to show them how much different it looked at night. She had been keeping an extra watchful eye on the comings and goings of the other sailors on the docks, and had been into town twice to check for word of any bounty hunters, but Samuel hadn't seen any yet.

Peridot was setting up her small

table near the gangway, laying out her Tarot cards and candles. Spinel was lighting red and white Chinese lanterns across the deck, Tanzanite was nearby walking along the railing of the ship. The twins were doing their practice swings on the main mast, their silhouettes outlined by the setting sun, making them look like flying shadows. Topaz was near the helm, playing his flute with Amethyst slithering in circles around his feet.

"Where can I set up shop, Miss?" Emerald asked, rubbing her hands together.

"We don't pick pockets on the ship, Em. Understand?" Mira told her seriously.

"Yes, Miss." Emerald replied, her voice dripping with disappointment.

"What do you think Zircon?" Mira asked. The woman had been strangely quiet throughout the tour.

"I think this is the most beautiful ship I've ever seen," Zircon said, turning to Mira and taking her hand. "Thank you, Mira. Thank you so much for bringing me to this wonderful place," She pulled Mira into a tight hug and started to cry.

Mira froze for a moment before taking Zircon into her arms, and she closed her eyes against the ache in her chest. When she opened her eyes a moment later, she saw Topaz looking at her over Zircon's shoulder. He quickly looked away and headed toward the gangway.

Four

Mira stood next to Peridot's
cushion as the fortuneteller counted the
coins that had been left on her table. She
wore her custom made monocle with
many lenses over her left eye. Her dress
had seen better days; it was skin-tight
now that she had grown a few inches
since she bought it. The enormous puffed
sleeves drooped and the bottom had
turned to rags. She refused to leave the
ship to buy a new one, and Mira refused
to purchase one for her. She carried her
father's pocket watch and had a habit of
flipping it open and closed when she was
nervous.

When Peridot was a child, she
would tell her parents that she could hear
and see things that weren't there. They
tried to keep her locked in their root

cellar, but she would scream and beat her fists against the door for hours on end, eventually a neighbor heard her and came to set her free. Her parents then changed tactics and made her read people's cards and contact their departed loved ones, charging an enormous sum and keeping it for themselves.

Mira had found her in a town square, reading palms for pennies; she was rail thin and wore an oversized black gown with a black veil covering her face. Her mother stood close by and would hit her with a switch if she asked for food, drink, or a break. Mira had paid her mother for a private séance on her ship, and sailed away with her that very evening. Now she refused to leave the ship under any circumstance, because she was afraid that her mother would be at port waiting to drag her home. She somehow managed to find the goodness in every member of the crew, and Mira admired her for it.

"I still can't believe that she chose to dance after everything she has been through," Peridot said.

"I can't either," Mira replied. "But isn't that the way of things? You still read fortunes, the twins still swing, Topaz still charms his snake and Spinel still makes Tanz jump through hoops. We stick with what we know."

They both grew silent after that, each lost in their own pasts.

Mira was about to speak again when a man pushed his way past several people waiting in line, paused briefly to read the hand painted sign posted at the top of the gangway:

Pay and be read to enter

He let out a booming laugh and yelled loudly for all to hear, "I ain't having this witch touch my hands, she would just as soon snatch off my rings than read my fortune!" The men crowded behind him laughed.

"Here," he said, dropping a handful of coins onto the table, "Have a few extra coins and lets skip the reading, eh?" He laughed again and strutted past Mira, giving her a long once over and turning back to his friends.

Mira gave him a once over herself. The man was short, but carried himself as if he were ten feet tall. He had thinning gray hair and a mustache that reached his ears. His arms and neck were covered in dark swirling ink and he had enormous rubies in each lobe. Everything about him demanded to be looked at, but the thing that caught her eye the most was the man's teeth. They were gold, shined to perfection, and the front two had diamonds set into them. She wondered how he could eat with teeth like that.

"I don't like the smell of that man," Peridot said, biting into a rather fake looking coin.

"As long as he minds the rest of my rules I don't care what he smells like," Mira replied, watching the man wearily.

She looked about, wondering where Spinel and Tanzanite, her lion, were lurking. It was likely that Spinel needed to oil her arm before their next performance, so she was up near the ship's wheel where customers weren't allowed. She hoped the man and his gang wouldn't need to be reminded of that rule as well.

"Hold tight," she told Peridot, "I'm going to make my rounds." Mira loved watching the faces of the crowds as they watched her friends perform, she was glad that their skills could be admired by so many and that they had a safe place to display them. She neared Peridot's table again and was laughing as she watched Emerald and her parrot were mimicking each other's movements when suddenly Topaz was beside her.

"Come quickly," he rasped, then turned and headed below deck without looking back to see if she was following.

"It will be about that man," Peridot called after her, flipping down one of the many lenses of her monocle. "I did warn you."

Mira let out a huff of irritation and took off at a leisurely pace as to not give the other customers reason to worry. It wasn't like Tope to come above deck while they were performing, so it must be something serious. The twins saw her following Topaz and stopped their swinging to watch. They had four swings attached to the main and aft masts of the ship and it was their job to keep an eye out for trouble while they were performing.

When she reached the cabin where Zircon and Tope were supposed to perform, Topaz and Amethyst winding around each other in an other worldly way, and Zircon dancing, she frowned. They were nowhere to be seen. She was about to turn back to the stairwell when something caught her eye. Zircon's collar lay crumpled on the ground near the side of the room, close to the false door that led to her sleeping room. Mira picked up the collar and thrust the door open, inside Amethyst, Tope's python, curled slowly around one of Zircon's wrist, flicking her tongue at the woman's face.

Mira took in her appearance; the front of her dress was torn open, one of her cheeks was red as if she had just been struck, and there was a trickle of blood dripping from her nose. Mira tightened her grip on the collar.

"Who did this to you?" She breathed.

Zircon looked down and wiped the blood from beneath her nose. Tope entered the room and looked between the two women, he didn't wait for Zircon to answer.

"That man with the teeth," he said as he snapped his own, Mira noticed that his bottom lip was swollen. "He came in here like he owned the place and grabbed her. I tried to stop him but his goons came at me from behind and pinned me down." His eyes burned with rage, "They left this."

He handed her a poster with a

large drawing of Zircon in the center, with the words: Missing Woman above it.

"Lock down the ship," Mira said coolly, never taking her eyes from the poster.

Tope uncoiled Amethyst from Zircon's arm and leapt up the stairs, yelling at the rest of the crew to secure the ship.

Zircon wouldn't meet her eyes; her hands had started to tremble as she tried to pull her gown tighter around herself.

"I'll have his head," Mira whispered as she got to her feet.

She could hear shouts coming from above her; no doubt the little man was trying to get off the ship before Mira could return. Everyone had heard about her reputation and what she did to patrons that misbehaved on her ship, no one had been foolish enough to challenge it for many years. As she reached the deck the shouting stopped, all eyes swiveled in her direction as she unsheathed her short sword. She pointed it at the little man and he puffed up his chest.

"What's this about?" He spit. "Let me off of this before I lose my temper."

Spinel cracked her whip at his feet and he jumped back.

"Get that freak of yours on her own leash before I do it for you!" He shouted at Mira, "And get that oversized house cat out of my way before I put a bullet in its head." He took a pistol out of his belt, but before he could point it at Spinel and Tanz, Mira loosed a dagger that struck him in the hand. He dropped the gun with a cry and savagely turned on her.

"You bitch!" He cried and clutched his hand to his chest. She took three quick steps forward and thrust her sword into his throat, silencing him before he could utter another curse. The men he was with stood in stunned silence as she ripped the sword from his neck and he fell to the deck. She wiped the blade on the back of his coat, flipped him over and took out her favorite dagger, then opened his mouth and cut out the two enormous diamonds from his teeth. One of the men wretched and she threw a glare at him.

"Clean that up," she told him, then, to the others, "To the plank."

They all slowly shuffled over to the side of the ship, some still staring open mouthed at her and the man she stood over.

"It's fine, we can just swim around to shore and get the rest of the boys," one of them whispered to the others. A loud crack sounded and the man fell. The rest looked up in surprise as Mira lowered the pistol she had taken from the little man's belt.

"I wouldn't make her repeat herself," Peridot said as she crossed to stand at Mira's side.

"I told you I didn't like the smell of him," she mumbled, watching the men swiftly climb onto the plank.

"Face me," Mira bellowed at the men. They were all too stunned from seeing her murder their leader to do anything but listen. But as they turned she raised the pistol to shoot, they began to jump on their own.

She turned to see that the last man was staring wide eyed at her on his hands and knees. She swiftly walked over to him and held her dagger to his throat, he started mumbling a prayer and she silenced him with a look.

"Go and tell the rest of your *boys* what happens when they touch one of my crew," she whispered, and then shoved him back to reveal that he had pissed himself as well. She made a sound of disgust and kicked him.

"Get off my ship!" She bellowed,

"Make sure I never see your face again."

The man scrambled to the gangway and almost fell off its side in his haste to leave. All eyes turned her way as she stood looking after the man.

"Make ready, we leave port in one hour," She said and turned to go below deck.

"But Cap-" Spinel started, but a glare from Mira silenced her. The crew shared a look and began to make their way about the ship, making preparations to set sail.

"We haven't even been in port a full day, we need to resupply-" Peridot tried.

Mira whirled on her, "Do not tell me what my ship needs, I said make ready." She turned her back and fled down the steps, faster now. She heard a muffled "Aye, captain," and rolled her eyes.

She paused and took a deep breath before slowly opening the secret door to Zircon's room. She shut the door quietly behind her and turned to face the newest member of her crew. Zircon was now seated at her small mirror table, cleaning the rest of the stage makeup off of her face.

"I heard quite a rumble going on up there," she said without turning around, "I hope you didn't kill all of them because of one ignorant man."

As an answer, Mira tossed the teeth she had just cut free onto the table and sat heavily on the bed. Zircon stared at them for a moment before turning around to face her captain. They looked at each other for a long breath before Mira finally spoke.

"I told you that if you chose to sail with me, I would protect you," she said, her voice barely above a whisper. "Tell me what he did to you."

Zircon turned to her, searching her eyes before she spoke.

"He told me my father sent him as a warning to go home willingly before I'm forced back," she whispered.

Mira looked at her for a long moment, then took her face in her hands, stroking her cheek with a thumb.

"I will not allow it," she told her quietly, "We will be leaving soon, we shouldn't have stopped so close to your home port."

She stood to leave but Zircon held fast to her hand. "Stay with me," she whispered.

Mira wavered for a moment, then carefully settled in beside her, stroking her hand until she fell asleep. She hadn't been this close to anyone but Topaz before and it felt strange to her, she had a warm sensation growing in her chest that she hadn't felt for a long time. She couldn't help herself; she leaned forward and planted a kiss on Zircon's wet cheek, and pushed her hair back over her ear. Soon she felt her own eyes drooping and fought sleep for as long as she could, eventually she gave in, still curled around Zircon.

She woke a short time later to a hand gently shaking her arm. It was Spinel, standing over her with an uncertain look on her face.

"We're ready," she said in that low tone of hers.

Mira gently pulled her arm from under Zircon and stood, she avoided Spinel's gaze as they turned to leave. Everyone on the ship knew that Mira and Topaz had been each other's companions ever since Mira freed him from that tavern all those years ago. They had grown to be great friends, and eventually more as time wore on.

Mira had refused his marriage

proposal more than once, stating that they didn't need rings and a piece of paper to tell each other how they felt. Topaz was very transparent with his feelings towards Mira, but she wasn't as good at showing hers for him. They had separate cabins but often spent their nights together, often on deck, huddled under a rough blanket and counting the stars until they fell asleep.

As Mira and Spinel reached the deck, Topaz was nowhere to be seen. Spinel noticed Mira looking and cleared her throat.

"He was the first one that went to fetch you, he is in his cabin now," she said, still not meeting Mira's gaze.

"Very well," Mira replied, reaching the ship's wheel, and giving it a hard jerk. "All hands to stations! I want this port well behind us before those sorry mongrels are missed," she bellowed, and the ship began to move.

Two days later, Topaz was still avoiding her. She couldn't blame him, she had broken their unspoken promise and knew she should apologize but couldn't bring herself to do it. He went about his business as if she weren't there, waiting for her to come to him. They were both too stubborn and pigheaded to make the first move, so Spinel made it for them. She requested that Mira meet her in her cabin because she had something very important to discuss with her.

When she arrived, Spinel sat her on her bunk and told her she would be back in a moment. Mira knew something was up the second the door was closed; she heard a distinct *click* and knew she had been locked in. She sighed heavily, crossing her arms to wait for whatever was going to happen next. She didn't have to wait long; she soon heard footsteps approaching and Topaz's deep voice, asking something she couldn't make out. Mira rolled her eyes; she really should have seen this coming.

Spinel opened the door, shoved Topaz in, and slammed it closed with more force than was necessary. Topaz eyed Mira sitting on the bunk and promptly turned around, he flung the door open to find Tanzanite prowling in the corridor, the lion turned to him and let loose a low growl. Topaz rolled his eyes and closed the door again, there was no use trying to get past the beast, he was far better at guarding something than any guard dog. He turned back to Mira and lifted a brow.

"You know I didn't set this mess up," she said to the floor.

"Oh I know Mira, it would mean you cared," he told her, his voice was calm but she knew he wasn't. Topaz was far more in touch with his feelings than she was, he could admit when he was hurt, she preferred finding a nice chunk of wood, or flesh, and applying a knife to it, pretending it was her feelings.

They stayed quiet for a tense moment before she finally gave up. She stood, arms still crossed, and slowly approached him. He stayed where he was and stared at her, hands on his hips.

"I don't know what to say to you, that's why I haven't said anything," she started quietly. When he didn't reply she went on.

"We both know that I care about you, I have for a very long time. I know that you care for me as well. I don't know what to do. I think I care for her in the same way-" she trailed off, not sure what else to say now that her heart was out in the open.

Topaz stayed very still for a heartbeat, then let out a loud sigh.

"Jesus, Mira, twelve years we've been together." He whirled around at her noise of disagreement. "Don't start that again. We *have* been together Mira. Don't tell me we haven't. Do you know how many women have made advances on me? I'll tell you. More than I can count, and I didn't even spare a glance in their direction. Because of you. Now what? Some twit shows up and gives you puppy dog eyes and now you've changed your mind about us? Or was your mind ever made up? Do I need to remind you that you threw a blade at my head last week for the same thing you did last night? Tell me how that makes sense. Were you jealous? You wanted to be the one snuggling up to her, not me? " He moved right in front of her so she was forced to look at him.

"Tell me Mira, tell me now so I know the truth," he looked from her mouth to her eyes, searching them for his answer.

She let out a small puff of air, "Tope, I- I do care for you, I just don't know-"

He turned and stormed out the door, leaving Tanz startled enough to leave him alone. Spinel sat on a wine barrel a short distance away, oiling her arm, she slowly shook her head as Mira passed her, not needing to say anything. Mira hurried to follow Topaz up the steps and onto the deck, his long legs and anger made him take the stairs two at a time.

She found him leaning against the railing staring across the water. She hung back a ways, still thinking of how she might put her feelings into words. She grimaced at the thought, she knew she loved him, but she also knew that she had new feelings for Zircon. Damn these feelings of hers. She did know of one sure-fire way to let Tope know how much she cared for him, so she opted for that option. She would figure out what to do with the rest of her heart later.

She approached him slowly, taking her hands out of her pockets and twisting her hair into a knot atop her head. When she reached him she put her hands on his waist and then slid them up his spine, nestling up to his backside. He stiffened at first but slowly relaxed, but still kept his back to her. She slid her hands to his chest and pulled him to her, he was a good deal taller than her so she rested her cheek on his shoulder. She rubbed his chest slowly as she turned him to face her, kissing a trail as he did. He let out a small sigh and put his arms around her shoulders.

"This doesn't mean I forgive you," he growled into her hair.

"Yes, it does," she replied, tilting her face to his and continuing her trail of kisses up his jaw. He groaned again and pulled her mouth to his. Their hands slowly explored each others body's as their kisses became hungrier. Mira tugged at Topaz's breeches and he groaned into her mouth.

"Don't you think we should discuss what happened with Zircon?" He asked her.

"I know what I am going to continue doing, you may discuss anything you like while I do it," she told him, hooking her forefingers into the tops of his breeches and bringing his lower half closer to her.

"Damn you, woman," he mumbled., sinking his teeth into her lower lip.

"I thought we agreed you wouldn't call me that?" She asked him.

"Very well," he said grabbing her by the hips and placing her roughly onto the railing, she hooked her ankles around his bum and forced him closer. "Damn you, *Madam,* "he said as he tore her shirt open.

"Much better," she replied, smirking. "Now, do that thing I like."

The next day, Topaz strutted around the ship like a peacock on parade. He whistled and hummed, driving everyone within earshot insane. He also left his shirt in his cabin, displaying his fresh scratches and other love marks proudly. The rest of the crew laughed at him and his more than positive attitude. Everyone had assumed the mess was cleared up and there were no longer any issues. Everyone except Peridot, that is.

She was as gifted in reading the stars and seas as she was reading one's future, so she was the obvious choice for the ship's navigator. She often took to the wheel when Mira was otherwise preoccupied; she had in fact been at the helm the night before when the two lovebirds were, quite literally, on the deck. She was seated near the ship's wheel now, a map lay over her lap, while Mira took over.

Peridot watched Topaz carefully, looking between him and Mira occasionally.

"What?" Mira grumbled after the

third time she had caught her looking.

"Out with it," Mira practically barked.

"The girl will be the death of him," Peridot said, nodding toward Zircon.

Zircon had emerged from below deck around midday, eyes still puffy from crying. She had obviously heard what had happened the night before, for she was doing her best to ignore Topaz and made sure to stay at the opposite end of the boat from Mira.

Mira let out a huff of annoyance. "She won't. I will sort out this mess and figure out what I need to figure out," she said, unsure of how to explain what was happening inside her head.

"That isn't what I mean," Peridot started, "There is a cloud over him that is linked to her. Something terrible is going to happen between them, something that will scatter us all to the winds." She had kept her eyes on Topaz while she said this, but looked Mira in the eye as she said this.

Mira shuttered at the sight of her friend's eyes, whenever Peridot was performing a reading or having a premonition, her eyes glazed over so much that she almost looked blind. Mira

looked away quickly. Now she had
another thing to worry about.

Five

Word of what Mira had done to the men coming after Zircon had spread, and they needed to get further away from her home port quickly.

They hadn't been properly out to sea since Peridot's rescue some eight years before, preferring to stick as close to the shoreline as possible. It was hard enough to operate a ship with such a small crew. No one was sure that the old ship would be able to take the wrath of the open sea and were all on edge as Mira drove them further and further from the coastline.

To make matters worse, Zircon had apparently never been on open water and spent every waking moment throwing up all over the ship. After a few days of this, Mira tied her waist to the main mast and her hands to a bucket so she could keep her mess more contained. She than enlisted Emerald to sit near her and bring her wine and broth when she thought she could stomach it, which wasn't often.

The young girl could be heard singing to her, telling her sea stories, and holding her hair back if she had a particularly bad bout sickness. Her bird was usually nearby, picking at peanuts or stretching its wings, never daring to get too close to Zircon or the bucket.

On the ninth day in the open sea, Mira was at the helm with Peridot and Topaz by her side, going over charts and trying to determine where the safest place to land was, when Aventurine, the ship's cook, came above deck. Mira knew right away that something must be wrong, Aventurine usually stayed below deck when they were sailing due to her sensitive skin.

"Here comes death Herself," Tope mumbled and set off in the opposite direction. The two had never gotten along very well. She considered it unlucky that the crew was mostly made up of women and hated the fact that the only two men aboard were either engaged with someone else, or her twin brother. It was clear that she was lonely and bitter to the fact that Mira had taken a lover, but no one else could.

"Captain," Aventurine said when she was close enough, "We're nearing the end of our fresh food. You haven't allowed me to properly restock in quite some time."

"I'm aware, Aventurine," Mira told her in a clipped tone. "No one has been allowed to restock in quite some time. We're all making due."

"We cannot go on like this," she pressed, "We only have one freshwater barrel left. We need to head back in. I also think we should give the girl back." She nodded her head toward the main mast, where Zircon was making excellent use of her bucket.

Peridot covered a laugh with her hand and flipped a glass on her monocle down. Mira could have stabbed her; she was far better at this type of thing than Mira was.

"Thank you for voicing your concerns, please see to it that our food supplies last for at least another week. We will be making port soon enough and everyone will be given the chance to restock," Mira told her in her best Captain's voice. She could handle ruffians and thugs, but she couldn't handle a disgruntled crewmember. She would have to ask Peridot what that meant later.

"That girl will be the death of us," Aventurine said coolly and turned to go back below deck.

A chill went up Mira's spine at those words, and she saw Peridot stiffen out of the corner of her eye.

Another week had gone by when Peridot sought out Mira, looking grim. When she found her, she was tied off from a railing and scrubbing barnacles off of the side of the ship. Peridot leaned over the rails and gave a loud knock. When Mira finally pulled herself back up over the side, Peridot passed her a small hip flask.

"What?" Mira growled, grimacing as she gulped down the foul liquid. "I was in my thinking place, you know I like to be left alone when I'm down there."

"You say that as if it's a tea room," Peridot replied, she let a small laugh and then grew serious. "Something is coming," she said quietly, "There is a shadow over the ship." Mira looked down at her hands, she was shuffling her tarot cards, a habit Mira knew meant that the other woman was extremely nervous.

Mira closed her eyes to this and took another gulp. "What sort of something?" She asked, handing back the flask.

"I'll let you know when I know," was all she said before heading back to her cabin.

"Well that was ominous," Mira said and she untangled herself from the ropes.

"We need to make port. Now," Topaz said.

"What is it now?" Mira asked.

"Emerald is sick with fever. She needs a doctor," Topaz said.

Mira stilled, "Have Per take a look at her, use those fancy herbs she's always having us collect for her."

Topaz grabbed Mira's shoulder and spun her around to face him. "She has been for hours now. This is serious Mira. She needs to go ashore."

"Very well," Mira said, turning toward the helm. "Drop sails!" She bellowed, "Hoist the anchor and make ready! We're heading for land!"

That evening they arrived in a small port, there was only one dock in which to tie off to, and she couldn't make out much more than three crumpling shacks haphazardly leaning against each other some fifty feet from the shore.

"This is the place?" Mira asked Topaz. After she agreed to go inland, Tope had set about looking for a port he remembered from their early days that had a well-known healer. They both had needed her help after they had had a particularly nasty run in with some smugglers they were trying to steal from. She had helped them and kept their secrets, they paid her in stolen gold and told her they would return to her if they ever needed help again.

"Yes, remember the rock I dived off of after she stitched my forehead?" He asked her, pointing to a large rock that was jutting out of the sea.

"She was so mad at you," Mira laughed.

"Well she had to stitch it again, I would have been upset too," Tope said. He was smiling down at Mira for the first time in what seemed like forever. They looked at each other for a moment more before Topaz cleared his throat.

"I'll go ahead and see if she is still here, she was ancient the first time we came, hopefully she isn't dead." He set off down the gangway so Mira went to gather Emerald and some of her things.

Topaz came back a short time later with the old woman close on his heels; she held a lamp above her head and looked over the crew that had gathered on deck to see Emerald off. Her eyes lingered on Zircon for a heartbeat longer than Mira felt comfortable with and Mira stepped into her line of sight.

"If you help the girl, we will pay you just as we did the last time we were here," Mira told the woman.

The old woman's eyes looked from Mira's to Emerald's to Zircon again. She nodded her head turned to leave.

"You will help her here," Mira said, suddenly afraid to let any of her crew out of her sight.

The old woman turned slowly, shaking her head. "I need my supplies," she said with a voice that sounded like gravel. She nodded toward the small village.

Mira gulped and looked around at the faces of her crew, they all looked back at her, waiting for her orders. She nodded her head.

"I will go with her," Spinel stepped forward, holding Emerald in her arms.

Mira nodded again.

"I will go as well." Topaz said. Mira didn't like the look of the bag slung over his shoulder, but she nodded anyway.

Silence descended upon the ship after they left. Mira stayed up long into the night, watching the path from the dock to the village. At daybreak, Citrine came to relieve her. She crawled into her bunk and sunk into a deep but fitful sleep, only to be woken what felt like moments later to a hand on her forehead. She peeled her eyes open to see a worried Peridot looking down at her.

"What is it?" She asked.

"It's afternoon, I just came to see if you were alright," Peridot said. She sat on the bed next to Mira and looked around the cabin.

"You should really clean this place," she said. She kicked aside the breeches Mira had dropped this morning.

"Let's go up and check how things are going, this place is giving me a knotted stomach," Mira said as she stood.

Peridot raised her brows in

amusement. "Did I just hear the famous Mira Tourmaline say a tiny port is making her uneasy? This place makes you nervous but nothing else does?" Peridot asked. Her brows furrowed as she watched Mira holster two pistols. "But you and Tope have been here before, you said it was safe."

"Nowhere is truly safe," Mira said.

When she reached the deck, Mira strode straight to the main mast and rung a small bell that meant she wanted whoever was in the crow's nest to come down, to her surprise Aventurine dropped before her.

"Six men rode in to town twenty minutes ago, Citrine went in to scout them out."

Fear seized Mira's heart and she took off in a run. "Guard the ship!" She called over her shoulder.

She reached the sunken hut on the other side of the village in time to see the horses riding away. She kicked the door in to find Emerald tied to a small cot in a corner and the old woman holding a knife over Topaz's lifeless body.

"No!" She roared, taking out one of her pistols and shooting the woman in the chest. The old woman's eyes went wide with surprise and she clutched her chest as she fell, Mira kicked her away from Topaz and knelt over him. He was alive but unconscious; someone had hit him over the head with something. She would kill them.

"A girl for a girl." The old woman croaked. Mira turned to find her leaning up on an elbow; blood was caked to her teeth. The old woman spit and repeated, "A girl for a girl."

Mira whirled around and realized what the woman meant. Spinel was nowhere to be seen.

Six

"He arrived just after you left, Captain," Citrine said. The rest of the crew was gathered on the deck of the Oddity's Revenge, looking down at a man that had delivered instructions for Mira: Meet them at a large palm tree grove two miles outside of town at dusk to exchange Zircon for Spinel.

Citrine and Aventurine had lassoed him with a rope as he tried to ride away, then tied him to the main mast to wait for Mira's return. They had used the man's horse to return to the hut and bring Topaz and Emerald back to the ship, the old woman was gone by then.

Mira paced in front of the man, looking down at him while he glared up at her. She dropped in front of his face and used a dagger to cut the rag that had been tied around his mouth. He spit at her as soon as it was off. Mira glared at him and stuck the dagger into his thigh. He screamed in pain as she used a rag to wipe off the spit.

"Tell me where your camp is," she demanded calmly, replacing the rag into her pocket. The man only continued screaming, so she twisted the knife. He let out another great cry and pissed his pants.

"Citrine," Mira called, "It would appear that I need a bucket."

Peridot turned away from them, taking Zircon and Aventurine below deck. Zircon looked back at Mira and Mira shook her head.

"You don't need to see this," Peridot said to Zircon.

Citrine brought Mira a bucket of seawater and tipped some over the man's leg. He let out another wail and Mira shoved the rag that had been tied around his mouth into it.

"Don't open your mouth again unless it's to tell me what I need to know," Mira hissed.

She retched his head back and dumped

the rest of the water onto his face. He spluttered and gagged into the rag, fighting hard against the ropes that tied him to the mast.

Mira ripped the rag from his mouth, "Tell me where she is," she screamed into his face.

The man looked down at the knife in his leg and back up at Mira. He looked like he was about to speak, but shook his head instead.

"Now is not the time to be brave, friend," Citrine said from behind her. "Tell my Captain what she wants to know, and I won't toss you into the sea with your hands tied to your feet."

The man bit his lip and shook his head again.

"Very well, I haven't been able to test the quality of this blade yet, now is as good a time as any." She slammed a fist into the knife and it sunk further into his leg.

He let out an earsplitting scream and started sobbing. "Stop! I'll tell you! They're three miles south of the grove. They are planning on keeping her there until dusk. They're planning to kill you! The girl's father said he would pay us triple the posted reward if we bring him your beard." He gulped down air, and looked at Mira with pleading eyes. "Let me go, please! I won't go back to the other men. I'll go north to the next port. Please!"

Mira looked over her shoulder at Citrine; he nodded once and left to gather his weapons. Mira turned back to the man.

"Coward." She said, and plunged the knife into his chest. She left him tied up as she dragged his body to the railing and dumped him overboard.

Citrine appeared then with guns strapped to his hips and a short sword across his back. He handed Mira her own, she nodded her thanks and they turned to leave.

They crept along the large palm trees outside of the camp, listening for the men. They had come across one lone sentinel and knocked him unconscious.

"If they were smart, they would post more sentinels," Mira said, mostly to herself.

Citrine stopped and pointed to the top of a tall tree, Mira nodded and bent to one knee. She kept watch as Citrine stepped onto her knee and shimmied up the tree. She could hear men's voices from inside the large canvas tent, laughing and yelling loudly. She would kill them all if they hurt Spinel.

Citrine slid down next to her, "There is one other sentinel on the far side. Looks to be either drunk or asleep. I counted three more horses, they don't seem to be missing the man that came to the ship."

"They probably knew I would kill him." Mira said.

She stood up and walked straight to the tent, throwing open the flap and startling the two men inside. She looked around and spotted Spinel bound and gagged in a corner next to an awful smelling bucket. She had a black eye and some blood dripping from the gag in her mouth. Spinel made eye contact with Mira and gave a single nod.

"Untie her," Mira said, not taking her eyes from Spinel's.

The men laughed.

"Well now!" One said, "Looks like old Bill gave away the location of our little camp, just like I hoped he would." He took slow steps toward Mira. "Did you bring any friends?" He asked, looking toward the tent flap behind Mira.

"I said untie her," Mira told him. "I'll give you to the count of five."

The man turned back to his companions and laughed again, but this time he laughed alone. The other two had clearly heard of her reputation before. They looked uneasily at one another.

"One," Mira began. No one moved.

"Two," she continued, looking back at Spinel.

The man before her let out a bark of laughter, "I'd like to see what you think you can do to the three of us all by yourself."

"Three," Mira said and took the short sword from her back.

The two men in the back simultaneously took a step backward. The man in front looked at them and whipped around to Mira. "I've had it with this," he said and took out his own short sword.

Citrine stepped in behind Mira; his pistol trained at the leader's head. "Four."

One of the men ran to Spinel and began to frantically untie her ankles. "Wait!" He yelled. The other man picked up a dagger but stayed where he was.

The man in front looked wildly between Mira and Citrine and the man untying Spinel. "Stop! Get away from her. Are you really afraid of these freaks?" He yelled at his men.

Spinel took her hands from behind her back, the rope falling from her wrists and pulled the gag from her mouth. "Bad choice of words," she said, then reared back and kicked the man in front of her square in the chest, sending him sailing into the table near them.

"Five," Mira bellowed and charged the man before her.

His eyes flew wide and he brought up his short sword just in time to stop Mira's from slicing into his head. Citrine fired a shot at the man in the back of the tent but it went wide. He charged forward and fired another shot.

"Stop firing!" Mira bellowed as her sword clashed with the man's, "You're going to hit one of us." She locked blades with the man and gave him a great shove, he tripped over a stool and his sword flew out of his hands. Mira leaped on top of him and drove her blade into his shoulder, he cried out in pain and kicked his legs out, bucking her off, and she lost her grip on the sword as she fell. Citrine ran toward the man and drove the sword in until the man stopped kicking, then wrenched it out and tossed it to Mira.

They turned to the last man together; he dropped his dagger and raised his hands. When they didn't move, he turned and ducked under the back of the tent. They could hear him yelling as he ran away through the sand. Spinel stood up after finally getting her ankles untied.

"That took longer than necessary," Mira told her.

"You try getting those blasted things untied when your hands are asleep," Spinel said. "Thanks for finally showing up by the way. Talk about taking longer than necessary."

Just then the second sentinel came in through the tent flap, he looked from the unconscious man and his dead leader, to Mira and her crew. He slowly started backing away when Spinel called, "Oh no you don't Rupert. I told you I would pay you back for this black eye." She strode from the tent and caught the man by the back of the shirt and pulled him down into the sand. She flipped him over and started beating him with her metal fist.

Mira counted to twenty and said, "Alright, either kill him or leave him. We need to leave. I smell rain."

Spinel stood and wiped sweat from her brow. She walked to Mira and they clasped forearms, metal and flesh.

"Thank you, Mira," Spinel told her.

"I will never leave my crew behind," Mira told her. Spinel narrowed her eyes, catching the double meaning, but nodded.

"Let's go," Citrine said, "Those clouds look deadly."

Seven

She gathered everyone at the helm and delivered her news. "From the looks of those clouds, I'm guessing the next few days will be rough. Hopefully we can outrun this, but we all know the Oddity isn't what she used to be. We need to prepare quickly. Secure your bunks, get the rain barrels tied off and set out our smallest net. With any luck we might catch some dinner for when this is over."

Everyone was quiet, glancing back and forth at each other. No one wanted to say what he or she was thinking: That the ship wasn't strong enough to survive a strong storm. They all turned, heading off in small groups to make their preparations. Topaz gave her a long look before his head ducked through the porthole.

When the storm hit in earnest, it took Mira, Topaz, and Spinel holding the wheel in an attempt to stay on course. They held on for what seemed like hours, eventually tying the helm in the direction they wanted and huddled together under a tarp. When the line snapped sometime later, they dropped anchor and tied up the sails, giving their fates over to whomever was looking after them.

"Get below deck!" Mira yelled to them, sensing a terrible turn in the storm.

They looked at each other; coming to a silent agreement then shook their heads at her.

"Now! There's no use in all of us catching our deaths up here! One of you can relieve me in six hours," she yelled again, the wind making it nearly impossible to be heard.

She knew that she would never let them be up here alone in this mess, but she had to say something to get them out of there. It took some more convincing, but they eventually gave in and agreed. Topaz giving her a fierce kiss and shouting something at her that she let the wind carry away. She couldn't think of that right now.

When they were gone, she tied herself to the helm, watching for a break in the storm, hoping she would be able to spot land. Topaz tried to relieve her sometime later, but she pointed her pistol at him the moment his head popped up from the hatch. They both knew that she would never fire it at him, but he got the message. He gave her a sad shake of his head and went back down below. They had made an agreement many years before that if the ship were to go down she wanted to be at the helm, she made him promise to let her go down with it.

She fought against the wind and rain, trying desperately to keep them on course. She brought out the compass Captain Ross had given her the day he died, and brought it to her face. It had always been a great comfort to her on stormy nights like this; it was as if he were there with her again, guiding the way. She attempted to wipe the worst of the water from its face when a wave rocked the ship and it slipped through her rain soaked fingers and rolled away. She cried out in anger and distress and began to weep, certain that they were doomed. But she was determined to get them back to land and cursed herself over and over again for being foolish enough to come this far out in the first place.

She couldn't be sure how much time had passed when she began losing consciousness, she opened her mouth to the rain in hopes that it would help her stay awake. Her eyes strained from being open for so long and from salt water constantly washing over them. Her body ached from being violently thrashed and from the ropes binding her to the wheel. She could feel something warm running down her side that she was sure was a cut from them, but when she looked down to check it was impossible to tell.

She closed her eyes and sent out a silent prayer that they would reach shore safely. She opened them again just in time to see an enormous wave heading straight for them. She was shaking from terror and the cold, screaming in time with the wind, and gripping the wheel with all of her might.

"If my time is now, let it be known that I have lived a full life! I have had the love of a great man and the comfort of a beautiful woman! I have had many hardships and seen my fair share of miracles! I shall greet death with a smile on my face!" She pulled free her favorite dagger and thrust it into the air. Come on you bastard! Do your worst!" She gave her fiercest war cry as the wave hit and knocked her into unconsciousness.

Below deck, the others had tied Zircon to her bunk, and gathered in the galley to wait out the storm together.

"We could take her up, leave her on the deck and let the storm have her, be done with this whole business." Spinel told them in a low voice.

Topaz and Peridot exchanged a long look.

"And what would you have us tell Mira? She would surely see us dragging an unconscious body up the steps and stop us," Citrine told her.

"That's if she can see us," Spinel cut in, "For all we know, she is unconscious herself. We could go have a look, act like one of us is coming to relieve her, if she is awake, then we don't go through with it. If she isn't, we throw that wretched girl overboard," she finished, eyes wild with the madness. "No on else needs to get hurt because of her.'

Everyone was looking at each other, silently going over the plan. When it seemed they had all decided, they looked to Topaz for approval. He cleared his throat.

"Should we throw this one over too?" He asked, pointing to Emerald. The young girl started, she still wasn't fully healed from her fever and sat slumped into the bench.

"What about these two?" He pointed to the twins, "I know Aventurine has been particularly annoying as of late," she scowled at him.

"We can't throw her overboard," Peridot said. "If we did, we might as well throw ourselves over as well. Mira would never forgive us for getting rid of one of our own. She would never hand one of us over, no matter the circumstances. You know what we mean to her." She looked around but no one would meet her eye. "You know that she is saving herself every time she saves one of us." She looked at each member in turn, staring until they met her eyes.

"I don't think we should give Mira the choice anymore," Aventurine started, she turned to Topaz and said, "I'm sorry but she is clearly infatuated with this woman for some reason. It's clear that her good judgment has gone away. We never should have taken that girl from that tavern. Peridot is the only one of us that has ever been well known before our time here and even her parents didn't come after her." She turned to Peridot, "I'm sorry, I am being cruel because someone needs to be. Someone needs to be logical about this; we *all* need to be logical about this. That girl is going to get one of us killed."

They were all quiet as this sunk in, they had all been thinking about it since Mira had killed the men in front of so many witnesses at their last port. She was becoming reckless.

Topaz was about to speak when the wave hit, sending them all flying around the room, crashing into the walls and each other. A stew pot knocked Emerald unconscious, Spinel lost a piece of her metal arm, and Citrine had a gash across his chest from a stray fishing pole. Everyone else seemed to be rattled but in good condition.

Topaz stood quickly, "Mira!" He bellowed, taking the steps above two at a time.

Mira woke up in her bed, the sea gently crashing against her porthole. She felt something move near her feet and looked down to see Amethyst, Topaz's python, curled in a knot. She smiled at this, attempting to sit up and hissed through her teeth as she did. She lifted her shirt, she was almost positive that it was Tope's, to see that her entire stomach was black and blue, and indeed had a large cut on one hip from the rope.

She took a deep breath and tried to sit up again when she heard a small laugh, she jerked her around to see Zircon sitting nearby.

"And I thought I was in bad shape," the woman laughed.

"Where are we? Is the storm over?" Mira rasped. Her throat felt like it had been coated in sand.

"The storm ended a while ago, the rest of the crew are up there," Zircon said, pointing up above them.   Mira could now hear footsteps overhead and what seemed like four giant paws running back and forth over the deck.

"How long have I been out?" Mira asked.

"Two days," Zircon said, moving to a small cask near the door. She pulled the cork out, and filled a tin cup with water and handed it to Mira. She drank it down in two gulps and handed it back.

"Why are you in here and not up there with everyone else?" Mira asked, her voice a little stronger now.

"I'm no use up there," Zircon said, not looking at her.

Mira took hold of Zircon's hand and held it tightly.

"Are you alright here?" She asked then more quietly, "Do you want to return home?"

Zircon sat for a moment, staring at her hand in Mira's. Her eyes began to swell.

"No, I do not wish to return to that place ever again," she whispered. "But I know the rest of the crew does not want me here any longer. They have made a point at pointing out how useless I am on the ship and how much attention I draw when we are in port. I know that it is very dangerous for you to keep me here, and I am very grateful to you." She paused, took a deep breath and looked Mira in the eye. "I want to stay here on the ship, I want to stay with you." She was looking at Mira's mouth as she said this.

Mira froze, her head and heart in two different places. Her heart demanded that she pull this woman onto her bunk and hold her tight, tell her everything would be alright, that she would protect her and keep her safe. That she could stay here as long as she liked, that she could stay with her. But her head was saying Topaz's name over and over again. She knew what it would do if she gave her heart what it wanted.

She cleared her throat and gave a curt nod.

"Then that is what you shall do, I will keep you safe as long as you are a part of this ship, just like I do with all of my crew," she told her, she tried to keep her voice hard like she did when she spoke with Spinel or Aventurine, but it faltered toward the end.

Zircon looked at her for a long moment and then said, "Thank you, Captain." Her voice was clipped, she was clearly as unhappy with Mira's response as Mira was.

Mira made a split decision that she thought she might regret later, but wouldn't now. "Come here," she said, pulling the woman's hand until it rested on her chest. They stared at each other for a heartbeat before Mira whispered, "Closer."

Zircon took a deep breath and laid down next to Mira, resting her head gently on her shoulder. Mira wrapped her arms around Zircon and held her as tightly as she could. They lay there, tangled around each other for sometime, not daring to move, too afraid of what would happen if they let their bodies take over.

Mira could feel Zircon's heart pounding against hers; it made her want to cup it in her hands and tell her everything would be alright.

"You would tell me if you were unhappy here, wouldn't you?" Mira asked quietly.

"Mira," Zircon began, "I'm not sure I will ever be happy on a ship." Mira stiffened and Zircon laughed. She rose onto her elbow and turned to Mira, her face only and inch or so away. "But I do believe that I could be happy anywhere, as long as you're around."

Mira let out a shaky breath, her lips parted to reply but all of her words were lost as she looked into Zircon's deep brown eyes. They were like the sea just before a storm. Zircon cupped her cheek in one hand and looked at Mira's lips.

"Would it be alright," she whispered, "if I kissed you?" She was slowly leaning forward, closing the distance between them. Mira gave a small nod, it was all she could manage, and closed her eyes.

It was the barest brush of their lips, but Mira felt as if an enormous weight had been lifted from her chest. She kept her eyes closed when Zircon pulled back, she could feel her watching her.

She opened her eyes and let out the breath she was holding to see Zircon smiling at her. She reached a hand up and brushed back a piece of hair that had fallen into her face. They stayed like that for a moment more, when there was a sudden tightening around Mira's feet. She let out a low laugh and looked down.

"I forgot we had an audience," she said and felt a stab of guilt at the sight of Amethyst. Topaz had clearly placed her there while he was elsewhere.

Mira cleared her throat, "Would you help me up? I need to check the ship."

Zircon's mouth turned down at the corners and she stood quickly, getting to her feet and clumsily helping Mira out of her bed.

It took longer than she would have liked, but they finally made it to fresh air. She saw that Peridot and Topaz were now at the helm, hunched over a map and compass. She was grateful that no one had noticed their arrival yet, she needed a moment in the fresh air to catch her breath.

"Bird girl," Peridot called out, without looking up.

Emerald's head popped up from drinking straight out of a rain barrel, she had an enormous bandage wrapped around her head and a black eye.

"I'm sorry Miss! I'm just so thirsty! I can't help it!" Emerald called back, her bird popped its head out of the same barrel and cried out, "Dar she blows!"

Peridot rolled her eyes at the pair.

"Shimmy on up to the crows nest and see if you can find land," she called back, "I'm having the damnedest time with these maps."

Emeralds eyes grew large.

"Up there, Miss?" She asked, pointing to the small bucket like stand at the top of the main mast.

"That would be it." Peridot called, still not looking up. "Why don't you check over the main sail too, while you're up there?"

Emerald stared at the rope ladder that ran up the main mast and gulped. Mira watched as Citrine walked over to the small girl and put a hand on her shoulder. She laughed as the girl jumped at his touch.

"Come now, it's not that scary." He said to her in his quiet way, and then motioned her to start up the ladder. "I'll be right behind you," he told her.

Emerald gulped again and started to climb, shaking all the way. About halfway up she faltered, letting out a startled cry as her leather slipper fell from her foot to the deck. She looked down to see Citrine giving her an encouraging smile and her ankle a small squeeze.

"Oh no, I can't watch this," Zircon said and went back below deck. Mira watched her go, she could tell that it wasn't just the thought of Emerald falling that drove her back to her cabin.

Mira was still watching them when Tanzanite brushed up against her leg, nearly knocking her over.

"Hello, you big Oaf," she told him lovingly, roughly rubbing her hand through his mane.

She looked around and saw a pile of boards near the gangway. She let out a frustrated sigh and added it to her mental list of repairs the ship needed. She had been hoping to get the to a port that had a well-known shipwright that was willing to make trades in exchange for his work. She hoped they weren't too far off from it now.

She was heading toward the railing to rest when a loud whistle sounded, she looked up to see Tope smiling wildly at her and her heart lurched again.

"Hang on tight, you Sea dogs!" He bellowed from the helm, "We're headed fast for land."

Eight

Mira was once again dawning her
rich man disguise. She was still stiff from
the ropes she used to tie herself to the
helm and it was taking her a bit longer to
dress herself. Emerald sat on her bunk,
facing the wall and told her of what she
had seen in town. She had been
dispatched as soon as they hit port to
ensure that the shipwright was still in
business and that there were no missing
person posters for Zircon.

"You won't believe me, Miss. Not in
a million years will you believe me!"
Emerald wriggled on the bunk, messing
up the worn blanket that Mira dutifully
folded each morning. Her head was still
bandaged and made Mira's hurt every

time she looked at it.

"Out with it, Emerald. I'm in no mood for guessing games, this shirt makes me itch." She made a mental note to buy a few more shirts; her supply was dwindling quickly thanks to them being ripped open so frequently as of late.

"There's a woman, Miss! She's as big as a tree! And her arms! Her arms are bigger than Topaz's! I swear it!" She whirled around suddenly and made a show of her nonexistent muscles, posing this way and that in an imitation of the woman she spoke of.

"Is that right?" She asked, her interest peaking.

"That's not even the strangest bit, Miss. She was strutting down the street in the prettiest dress I've ever seen! She had on those shoes that raise you up a few inches, not that she needed it! She had a pretty parasol draped over her shoulder like a princess! There was a whole crowd of people following her, yelling things that would even make you blush."

Emerald was growing louder and louder as her explanation went on.

"What was she doing?" Mira asked, she didn't like the sound of a crowd following this woman.

"She was just walking, Miss. Sort of like Topaz does some mornings. All strutting about like she's the belle of the ball." That comment made Mira's face hot, she knew exactly why Topaz acted that way some mornings.

"Good work, Em. Good work," she said, giving the girl a pat on the head.

Mira, Topaz, Spinel and Citrine made their way down the dock toward the town. They each had a list of supplies in hand and a destination in mind. Mira was off to discuss business with the shipwright who, thankfully, was still in business. Topaz and Spinel were off to restock the medical supplies, drinking water and wine. Citrine's list was by far the longest; it was a thoroughly detailed account of everything Aventurine would need for the galley: food, oils, spices, and a new stew pot since the last one had been thoroughly damaged by Emerald's head during the storm.

"Why couldn't she go after the food herself again?" Spinel asked, eyeing the list in question.

"She is taking Emerald to find a doctor," Citrine said curtly. They all grew quiet. Mira knew they expected her to apologize at some point, she just couldn't see the sense in doing so, so she hadn't.

As they approached the market stalls, they saw a crowd around a stall that advertised fine silks, thread and needles. They could hear a man shouting profanities as the rest of the crowd shouted their agreements.

The sailors all exchanged a look and sprung into action. Topaz and Citrine shouldered their way to the front of the crowd, making a pathway for Mira while Spinel wound her way around to the side. She slid her hands into her pockets as she reached the front and surveyed the scene. There was a short man waving a short club around in the air and occasionally beating it against his hand, spit flew from his mouth as he cursed the woman across from him.

Mira's brows rose as she saw the woman, she really was as big as a tree. She was easily a foot taller than the man working the stall, her hair was waist length and shined as if she brushed it three times a day. The dress she wore was indeed one of the finest Mira had even seen, it was baby blue with white lace trim and bows along the hem, it had obviously been tailored to fit her for it hugged her torso and arms perfectly. Her arms were bigger than Topaz's, a fact that Mira realized a second before him and had the pleasure of seeing his face when he realized it.

The woman was looking down her nose at the man in front of her, one hand still clutching the parasol on her shoulder and her other held a row of pink silk.

"I've the right to refuse to sell to whoever the hell I want!" The man was saying.

Mira took her hands out of her pockets as she saw Spinel walk up behind him; she was eyeing the club he was swinging with a ferocious look on her face.

"Tope," Mira said quietly, indicating that they should attempt to break up the fight.

"On it, Love," he replied, taking a step forward, but before he could do anything, the tall woman spoke.

"Sir," she said, her voice was quiet and as smooth as honey, everyone at the stall stopped whispering and watched what was about to happen.

"All I am trying to do is buy the silk. Take my money, and I'll be on my way." She reached into purse at her waist, took out a few coins and held them out to the man. He stared up at her, his mouth opening and closing like a fish.

She shrugged a shoulder, dropped the coins on the table and started to walk away.

"You just wait right there!" He shouted, coming out from behind his stall. Everyone parted as he went after her, eager to see what would happen.

He was forced to run to catch up to her and jerked her around by the shoulder, ripping the seam of her dress. Mira and the others hurried after him, ready to help the woman out.

"Didn't your father teach you any manners? It's clear you don't have a husband to teach them to you, who would marry a woman like you? Perhaps you, need to be taught again how to speak to a man," the man shouted up at her.

The tall woman slowly put a hand to her torn shoulder, took a deep breath and turned to the man. As she did, the man swung the club at her face but she caught one end and held it easily, leaning down into his face.

"I do not need anyone to teach me anything, little man. Perhaps you need a woman to teach you how to act in public. Now move out of my way or I will move you," she said quietly, shoving the club into his chest.

She turned, flicking her long hair over her shoulder, and sauntering away from him and the scene he had caused.

Mira looked over to tell the others how impressed she was, when she caught a glimpse of Citrine. He stood stalk still, one hand over his heart, and his mouth slightly open as he stared after the tall woman. Mira looked at him in confusion, had she missed something?

Suddenly, Spinel was at her side, chuckling.

"That's the way Topaz looks at you," she said, with humor in her voice.

"What do you mean?" Mira asked, looking back and forth between Topaz and Citrine.

"Come on, Cap. We had better go tell her what we're about so Citrine doesn't have to stay here with her," Spinel said as she started after the woman, shaking her head.

Topaz came up behind her, looking after the tall woman.

"Is she right? You look at me that way?" She asked him.

He let out a heavy sign and slung an arm around her shoulders.

"It's a good thing Per is the navigator, you never could read signs very well," he said to her.

Mira let out a huff of irritation and slipped out of his grip. She was annoyed because she really had no clue what he meant.

They caught up with the woman in no time, it had been very easy to follow her, not because of her height; but because Citrine was right behind her and all they had to do was follow the cloud of his hair.

She walked to the edge of town and stopped as if she was waiting for someone. The crew all watched as Citrine approached her, he gently touched her elbow and spoke for a few moments.

They all leaned against a low wall and waited to see what would happen.

"Do you suppose he is proposing already?" Spinel asked.

Topaz let out a chuckle, "If he hasn't I wish he would, I'm starving."

"You're always starving," Mira grumbled.

"Starving for you," he replied, with a cocky grin.

"Oh Seas," Spinel said, "I think I'm going to be sick. It's bad enough watching you strut about like a cock in a hen house, I don't need to witness the foreplay." She pretended to throw up over the wall and Mira turned bright red.

"If you think that's what foreplay looks like, I feel rather bad for you Spinel," Tope said, "I could give you a lesson if you'd like." He was grinning madly at the sight of Mira's embarrassment.

"Enough," Mira boomed, "I've had enough waiting, the more time we spend standing around, the more time the ship sits without repairs. Lets go see when the wedding is."

As they approached they could hear Citrine's low lint, but they couldn't hear what he was saying. He glanced back over his shoulder at them and gave them a shy smile.

"This is Queenie," he said, "I was just telling her about your ship, Captain Mira." He gave a small bow and moved aside so Mira could get a better look at Queenie.

Now that she was closer, she could see that the tall woman not only had a fine gown, but very fine jewelry and a thin piece of lace wrapped around her head. She looked more like a duchess than a woman from a fishing village. Her eyes were an impossible shade of cerulean, and she had a dusting of deep brown freckles across her nose that made her look like a young girl.

"Hello, Miss Queenie." Mira said, not trying to disguise her voice. "I am Mira Tourmaline, Captain of The Oddity's Revenge. This is Topaz, and that over there is Spinel." Topaz gave her a nod and Spinel waved her metal arm.

"It seems you've already met Citrine," she said with an amused laugh. Citrine turned pink and gave her an embarrassed smile.

Queenie's eyebrows had drifted lower and lower as Mira spoke, she looked from one person to the next, her gaze landing on Mira.

"Forgive me Captain, but you have an unusual voice and name," Queenie said.

Mira looked at Citrine, confused.

"I thought I'd leave you to tell her your business, Cap." He said with a nod towards her chest.

She cleared her throat, "Very well

then, as I said, my name is Mira, I am a woman and I also have a beard. Topaz is my first mate, he is also a snake charmer." At this, Topaz flashed his filed teeth at Queenie and her eyes grew wide.

"Spinel is our lion tamer," she said with a nod to Spinel.

Queenie let out a gasp, "Is that what happened to your arm?" She asked.

"Something like that," Spinel said.

Mira rolled her eyes and continued, "I'm assuming that Citrine told you about our ship? That we rescue other- people like us- and travel the seas?"

"Yes, he mentioned that," Queenie said, she didn't seem convinced that that was something one should brag about. "Who says that I am like you?" She asked, raising her chin a fraction higher.

They all stared at her.

"Right," Mira said, "Well, if you would like to see the ship for yourself and the rest of the crew for yourself, it will be open to the public tomorrow night. Have a nice day, Miss Queenie." Mira gave her a polite nod and turned to go, Topaz and Spinel coming with her. She glanced back to see Citrine kissing one of Queenie's hands and the tall woman blushing. She shook her head and continued on.

"She said that if we expect her to show, we had better be dressed a little better than we are now," Citrine said when he had caught up to them. "She also said your shirt isn't very tasteful." He told Mira with sideways glance.

"What is it with you people and my shirts?" She demanded.

The next evening, Mira stood at the helm of her ship and watched the comings and goings of the crowd, curious to see if Queenie would show. She had noticed that the twins brushed their hair and Aventurine had wound her plaits around her head like a crown, making them more distinguishable. Mira smiled at that, Citrine must want to make a very good impression on Queenie. Spinel walked passed just then and she noticed that her hair was always shiny, as was Tanzanite's. She raised a brow at Spinel.

"What?" Spinel asked, more question than statement.

"Why does your hair look like that?" She asked.

"It's called a wash," she replied, flicking her long curls over a shoulder. "Not all of us wish to have locks like you."

Mira tried not to take offense, dreadlocks were much more manageable. She liked only having to clean and re-roll them every few months.

"Are you trying to make a good impression on Queenie, as well?" She asked.

Spinel looked confused at this and glanced up to where the twins were currently swinging through the air, then shook her head.

"Not everyone needs a reason to clean up," she said and sauntered away.

After that bizarre encounter, Mira began her usual rounds about the ship, greeting the village folk that had come to see the ship and her crew, making sure they understood the rules and looking over them in case any looked up to no good.

She always liked to let a few curious children give her beard a tug to make sure it was real. It made her heart happy to see the few young girls that seemed to have a few dark hairs above their lips, they always looked at her in wonder, she made sure that they knew it was just body hair, and that everyone has it. She liked to think of herself as a role model for these girls.

A small boy squealed past her, looking terrified and shouting for his mother. Mira looked in the direction he had come from to see Spinel and Tanzanite standing there, a smirk on the woman's face.

As she neared the gangway, she noticed Peridot standing with her arms folded, looking unhappy.

"What is it?" Mira asked, instantly uneasy. She hoped desperately that no one had come looking for Zircon, they had come too far at too great a cost to leave now.

"That... *thing* told me I needed a new dress," Peridot grumbled. Mira turned her gaze to follow hers.

Across the ship, in all of her glory, was Queenie. Mira had almost forgotten that she was supposed to come tonight. Queenie's gown was now a deep plumb color, she had on matching lace gloves and a cloche with a large daisy pinned on the side. She was running a finger along the railing to inspect the grime that had gathered there.

"That would be Miss Queenie," Mira scowled at Peridot. "You know better that to use words like that on this ship." She headed off in her direction.

"Of course it is." She heard Peridot groan, then louder, "How many strays are we going to pick up this year Mira? We've never taken on this many so close together before. It's going to cause problems."

Mira closed her eyes; she could feel a headache coming on. Peridot was usually the voice of reason, as well as calm and kindhearted, but sometimes Mira thought she forgot where she had come from, and that she too had been referred to as a "thing."

"Good evening Miss Queenie, thank you for joining us," Mira told her with a tip of her top hat.

Queenie didn't reply right away. She was looking up where the twins were performing. Her eyes grew wide as Aventurine let go of her swing and went sailing towards her brother. He caught her with one hand, twisting her in tight circles before sending her sailing back to her own swing. Queenie let out a small gasp and started to clap loudly when Aventurine caught hold of the swing. The twins simultaneously pulled themselves up to stand on the swings, waving at the crowds below.

"Pretty amazing, aren't they?" Mira

asked her. She had always liked watching people's faces as they watched her companions doing what they loved.

"This place is pretty amazing," Queenie replied, still looking around the ship. "Even if it is quite dirty." She looked Mira up and down.

"It is lovely to see you again, I'm sure Citrine will be thrilled," Mira told her, clearly irritated.

"I'm sure," Queenie replied, turning her back to Mira.

Mira took a calming breath, "Have you given any thought to our proposal?" She asked when she caught up, Queenie's long steps were equal to three of Mira's short ones.

"I have been doing little else, Captain, but I have not yet decided what my answer will be. I must admit that the state of your ship is not helping me make my decision. Neither are the wardrobes of your companions," Queenie replied, clutching at her purse as they passed Emerald.

The girl and her bird were dancing circles around each other near the railing, a hat in front of them. A small crowd had gathered around them and Emerald was looking at the pockets around her with greedy eyes. Mira let out a low whistle and raised an eyebrow at Emerald, who had the good graces to look embarrassed and flashed a smile at her audience.

"Is your entire ship made up of criminals?" Queenie asked her, eyeing the girl.

"No, just the one," she replied with a chuckle, glancing around to make sure no one heard her.

"Excuse me Captain, I think I have seen quite enough. Please give my regards to Citrine." With that, Queenie turned and swiftly left the ship.

Mira was left standing alone with her mouth hanging open; she didn't know what just happened.

"Maybe you should have left that with Citrine," Spinel said with laughter in her voice.

The next morning, Mira awoke to a heavy fist hammering at her door. Topaz groaned next to her and shoved his head under the pillow. He had come in late last night and she hadn't the heart to refuse him. Her feelings for him were still there, but the more her feelings for Zircon grew, the more they shadowed the ones for Topaz. It was extremely irritating.

"The ship had better be on fire," he mumbled, pulling Mira to him.

"Could be someone after Zircon," Mira replied and closed her eyes shut, why had she said that out loud? Topaz let out a growl at the mention of the woman.

She tried to muzzle his cheek but he pushed out of bed, Mira could tell that he was growing more impatient with her by the day.

"If it is someone looking for her, I'll fetch her myself," he said angrily, and flung the door open.

Braced against the threshold was Aventurine, she was breathing heavily and had a murderous look in her eye.

"You," She boomed pointing at Mira, "You did this to him." She stormed into the room and tried to pull back the blanket covering Mira.

Mira sat up quickly and pointed her pistol at Aventurine's head.

"I've had about enough out of you, girl. First you try to tell me how to run my ship and now you barge into my cabin talking nonsense. You better have a good excuse for yourself, or I'll throw you off my ship. Your brother be damned," Mira told her, her voice dripping with venom. She would never kill one of her own crew, the gun wasn't even cocked, her finger wasn't on the trigger, but she would make a point by showing it.

"My brother is the one I am speaking of." Aventurine said, voice low. "You have planted that witch in front of him and now she is all he sees."

"What in God's name are you talking about, woman?" Topaz asked from the corner, he was pulling his clothes on, and Mira couldn't help but give him an appraising look.

"Come," Aventurine said, then turned and marched out of the room.

"There's never a dull moment on this damn ship," Mira mumbled, rubbing the sleep from her eyes.

They joined Aventurine on the deck, looking around and seeing no one. It was still very early and the rest of the crew was likely still sleeping.

"What is this about Aventurine? I don't see anything amiss out here," Mira was becoming more irritated by the moment and was eyeing the closest railing, wondering if she would need Tope's help in throwing the woman overboard.

Aventurine simply pointed toward the sky, one hand planted on her hip.

"Oh my stars and those who control the seas." Mira groaned, "Aventurine, I really hope you can swim as well as you can swing."

She stilled when she looked up and found what Aventurine was pointing at. Up the main mast sat Queenie and Citrine, they had the main sail piled in their laps; they seemed to be mending it. Their bare feet were dangling, and their heads were bent together, she couldn't remember the last time she had seen Citrine look so happy.

"What is happening?" Topaz asked, he stood as still as Mira and looked more shocked than she did.

Citrine spotted them and waved, then turned to Queenie and they spoke a few words. After a moment she nodded and they began the descent to the deck. They both landed with a thud and walked slowly over to the small crowd, Queenie's hand resting gently in the crook of Citrine's arm. Topaz and Mira stood silently, waiting for them to speak.

"I will join your crew," Queenie told them, looking deeply into Citrine's eyes. "Your ship needs me more than I realized."

Beside her, Aventurine sucked in a

breath and turned away, hurrying back below deck.

"Very well," Mira said, stunned.

"I have chosen a new name, as well. I am to be called Pearl now," she told them, her chin lifted.

"Pearl?" Topaz asked in disbelief.

"Is there a problem with Pearl?" She asked, looking down her nose at him.

"It's just not really a precious gem, that's all," he said quickly.

"It is precious to me," and with that, she turned her back and headed back to the main mast.

"Very well," Mira said again. It seemed to be all she was able to say.

Nine

After Pearl's unexpected arrival and trying to make accommodations for yet another new crewmember, Mira was worn out. Spinel offered to bunk with Pearl, but Pearl had refused, saying she would never be able to sleep knowing there was a lion lurking nearby. Peridot was the next option, but Pearl had refused her as well, saying the fortunetellers candles and incense would be the cause her to have constant headaches. The only option left was Emerald, seeing as how Zircon's room was barely large enough to fit her. They had moved Pearl's few belongings into the girl's cabin and Pearl promptly set out stitching hammocks for them to string across the space.

Mira was stretched out in her own hammock near the helm almost asleep when she felt someone give her a gentle push.

"This had better be good, I am trying to catch up on my beauty sleep," she told the intruder. She had a pretty good guess as to who it could be, most of the crew was either in town buying their bits and bobs, or below deck making the necessary repairs to the galley. The old shipwright had shown up earlier that morning and Spinel had taken over the role of repairman, showing the man the worst of the damage and striking a bargain to have it fixed.

The hand simply gave her another push in reply and she gave a heavy sigh, tugging up the bandana she tied around her eyes to keep the sun out. It was Topaz, giving her a devilish smile. She groaned.

"No. Whatever it is you're planning, no," she told him firmly, pulling the bandana back into place and folding her arms across herself.

"Come on Mira, we haven't had any fun lately," he replied, a smile in his voice.

"Right, stealing a woman out of a busy tavern, knocking out four men on a busy street, and killing, what was it? Five more? Taking on a street rat and her obnoxious bird. Then taking on an enormous woman who thinks she is the queen is just a regular Tuesday for us, is it?" She had been counting off each offense and stopped here and waited for his reply.

"Well when you say it like that..." Topaz mumbled.

"That is exactly how it is, so I wouldn't put it any other way, Tope," she said, exasperated. "Now if you don't mind, I have a nap to take."

She put her hands behind her head and pushed her bare foot against the rail of the ship, setting herself off at a gentle swing. She could feel Topaz standing nearby still, and waited for him to continue, but he didn't.

She heaved another great sigh and ripped the bandana off, sitting up.

"What are you scheming?" she demanded. He was leaning up against the railing, holding what looked to be a pink tent in his arms.

"What the devil is *that?*" She screeched.

He chuckled, slowly unfolded the thing in his arms and held it up. It was vaguely in the shape of a dress.

"This," he said, holding the dress out to her, "is a distraction."

"I'll have no part in it. I wouldn't be caught dead in that thing," She said, leaning away, and shaking her head.

"Oh, yes you will." Topaz laughed.

After attempting to fight off nearly the entire crew, Mira had been stuffed into the dress, Pearl had made the necessary adjustments, Peridot had done up her hair, and Zircon had fixed her makeup. Aventurine even came in at one point and offered Mira a set of her prized slippers.

She stood in Spinel's room, turning this way and that in front of a mirror someone had brought in and propped against a wall. She had to admit that she liked the way she looked. The dress wasn't all that terrible now that the enormous sleeves had been cut off, the waist was cinched to show off her slight curves, and the bosom was cut low enough to make her blush. Her feet were stuffed into slippers that were too delicate to house something as foul as a sailor's feet. It was far grander than anything she had ever worn before.

"Alright, now that I'm in this contraption, what is it for?" She demanded as the other women gathered around and gave their praises.

"You'll see," Spinel said with a sly smile, Mira noticed Spinel had been absent throughout the process of getting her ready, even though they were in her cabin.

Peridot took her by the hand and led her to the deck above. When they reached the last step, Mira looked up to see Topaz standing near the railing, she stopped for a moment to take him in. He was wearing a dark gray formal jacket that looked to be as tailored to him as her new dress was to her, new black breeches, a black silk shirt and what looked like brand new boots. She looked him up and down hungrily and he smiled.

"There will be plenty of time for that later," he told her, "Right now, we have somewhere to be." He reached a hand out towards her and she went to him.

"What is this all about?" She asked him.

"We're going to a party," he replied, tucking her hand under his arm and led her down the gangway.

They walked through the port, (she never could remember their names, that was Peridot's job) and she took the time to look around at the surrounding buildings. Most of them looked fairly new. It was bigger than most of the ports they visited, larger crowds usually meant more trouble, so they tended to stick to smaller, more inconspicuous ones. She also liked the intimacy of smaller crowds. You could show each patron a trick; give them each something to remember you by, if there were only ten or so watching you at a time.

As they neared the edge of the main street, a large stone house appeared in the middle of a small and well-kept garden. The yard was covered in rows upon rows of flower beds, three apple trees stood perfectly aligned with the edges and center of the house, the grass around them looked as soft as a cloud.

The house itself was a gray stone box three stories high, with more flower boxes at every window. It looked newer than most of the buildings in town and Mira thought to herself that whoever owned it must be very wealthy.

There was a gravel path that led from the low stonewall around the edge of the property, to the main door, and a few small groups of people in fine evening dress stood talking on the path. They all turned and stared at Mira and Topaz as they made their way up the path.

"Explain. Now," Mira whispered fiercely as they passed another couple.

He let out a huff of laughter and patted her arm. "Relax Mira. This is the house of the Duke or Lord of... something or another, I forget his name, but that is not the point. He and his wife have invited us here tonight for a dinner party. Isn't that nice? We've never been invited in by the village folk before. I did some asking around after receiving his invitation and found out that he is a very wealthy man with a very large collection of gems. I figured we could simply pick some up while we are here," he gave her his most dazzling smile and tightened his grip on her arm.

"You thought we would pull a heist while we are trying to keep a low profile? Not to mention the fact that we now have one of these townsfolk on our crew? What would she say if she found out we had stolen from this man?" Mira demanded; she couldn't see anything positive coming from this situation.

"Pearl, what an awful name for such a woman, has been so kind as to tell me where the gems are kept, and how best to sneak past the footman who stands guard outside the room," he said, looking straight ahead and trying his best not to smirk.

"She what?" Mira sputtered, "I don't believe this. You and Pearl planned this all without me?"

"The entire crew did actually," he said, looking at her out of the corner of his eye. "Close your mouth, you look like a fish. Yes, we all performed mutiny while you were tucked in bed. Get over it." He gave her a hard tug and she was forced to keep walking as they entered the house.

The room itself seemed to shift its eyes toward them as they entered. Couples turned to whisper or point, some openly stared at them. Mira and Topaz straightened even further, not making eye contact with anyone as they took a turn around the room. When a group of young girls next to them giggled, Mira turned her eyebrow up at Topaz.

"And exactly how are we to steal a gem with the entire house watching our every move?" She whispered, flagging down a footman that was carrying a tray of drinks.

"Oh I'm sure Emerald is already in the room," he said sweetly, flashing his pointed teeth at the young girls. They all gasped and turned away. He let out a low chuckle at the sight of them.

"I'm sorry I think I misheard you, did you say *Emerald* will be stealing the gem?" Mira choked out.

"No you heard that correctly, you did keep her because she is a thief did you not?" He asked.

"I did because you told me to." She turned to him, "If she gets caught this will be your fault, they will know that we are behind this. They will lock her up." She turned to leave and he caught her hand.

"Then we will have to make sure that no one finds out." He told her, then started dragging her toward the dance floor.

People parted around them as they moved into position, most of them left the dance floor so they could watch the strange spectacle.

When the music began, the noise around the room increased. Everyone was watching them as Topaz expertly led Mira through a waltz, some even smiled as they twirled near them.

Topaz pulled her closer when he felt her unease at being watched so closely. "Don't look at them, look at me," he told her. "They don't see you the way I do."

Surprised, Mira looked up at him, his eyes blazed with an intensity that she had not seen from him in some time. She felt her heart pound a little hard at the sight of them. She couldn't hold his gaze for long, so she looked at his lips instead. Guilt coiled in her belly as she realized they were a similar shape to Zircon's

One side of his mouth turned up and she was sure her face was reddening as she thought of the way both sets of lips felt against hers.

He must have sensed her unease because he pulled her to his chest and said, "No one will ever see you the way I do."

She closed her eyes and took a deep breath. The music had stopped and they were the only ones left on the floor.

"Tope," she began, "we need to talk about Zir-"

"I know everything about you, Mira. Did you think I wouldn't after all of this time?" He held her there, as the whispers grew louder. "I won't make you choose between us, mostly because I don't know what I would do if you didn't choose me." He let out a small laugh. "All I ask is that you leave room for me; leave room for all of us." He took her hand in his and led her through the steps of the dance.

"You look as if I have told you I have a tail," he told her after the song had finished.

"I think I would be less surprised about that." She told him, "I don't know what to think, let alone say."

He guided her off of the dance floor and got them both a small slice of cake. "You don't need to say anything, Mira. I have thought it over and I am willing to share you. No matter what you say or do, I will love you all the same," he told her softly.

She lost control of her fork and Topaz bent to pick it up. He was smiling as he stood.

"I know that I haven't told you that before, I also know that this isn't the time or the place to say it. But I thought you should know."

Mira stood there, eyebrows raised in shock. She didn't know what to think. First, her crew had planned a heist without her, with her as the distraction. Second, Topaz had practically told her that he was fine having an open relationship with her and another woman, a woman that she had feelings for. And now he had finally confessed his feelings for her. Yes, he had asked her to marry him many times before, but this something else entirely. This was love. She was certain she felt the same for him; she must after being by his side for so long. But what did she feel for Zircon? Was it love as well?

Her head swam while she tried to process all that had happened. She flagged down another footman and took two drinks from his tray, draining them both before he could walk away.

Topaz laughed and held out his hand. "Come, let's live our last night alone together to the fullest."

She took his hand and they headed back to the dance floor, laughing loudly as they danced a country-dance. They were each offered a dance with separate partners, which they accepted. Topaz's partner was a spritely old woman with a wig so high that Mira wondered how she could keep her balance. When Topaz accepted, the woman stepped far too close to him, raked her hands down his chest and dragged him to the dance floor. Topaz looked back over his shoulder with a pleading look that made Mira laugh out loud.

The gentleman who had asked Mira to dance was easily ten years younger than her. His black hair was tightly slicked against his head, and he had the shadow of a mustache growing above his lip. He gave her full beard an envious look as they took their positions.

"I let children tug my beard when they come to my ship, most of them think it is fake until they do," she said, smiling at him.

"Well, I am not a child, but I wasn't sure of its authenticity until I saw it up close. If it is fake, you did a remarkable job securing it to your chin." He responded; Mira's eyebrows shot up.

"You are very well spoken for one so young," she said, taking a better look at him, his suit was well made but did not fit him well, she thought it might belong to an older brother. He had a scar through his upper lip, and his hands were very rough, which Mira found suspicious of a gentleman.

When he didn't answer her, Mira said, "I'm sorry I seem to have forgotten your name, too much wine." She laughed. She started searching for Tope.

"I didn't give it," the man said. He took a firm hold on her waist, and leaned in to whisper into her ear. "I suggest you accompany me to the refreshment table." He let go of her and stalked off, leaving her in a sea of dancers. She spotted Tope and gave him a small nod. He looked like he was trying to follow her but the old woman wouldn't let him go, if anything she seemed to grasp him tighter. He gave Mira a shrug, so she followed the man alone, checking the blade she had hidden at her waist as she went.

The young man was busy gulping down a glass of wine when she reached him, so she picked up her own and waited.

"You're Mira Tourmaline," he said when he finished.

"Your observational skills are astounding," she told him, eyes trained on Topaz.

He scowled in her direction. "I've been following you for some time now, Miss Tourmaline." Mira's unease grew.

"Is that so? I didn't realize I had a fan club." She pretended to scratch her elbow, slipping the blade into her dress sleeve.

"I was hired by Miss Creed's father. He has paid me to bring his daughter home, along with your head." His eyes were trained on her now.

"I'm sorry, who?" Mira asked him sweetly.

"The new woman in your little freak show." Mira's grip on her glass tightened, "I went aboard last night and saw her myself, no wonder her father wants her back. I bet he rakes in all kinds of money with her being able to dance like that." He took a step closer to Mira and she straightened to her full height.

"Hand her over and I'll say I took her from the village. I don't see why a woman such as yourself has to succumb to the pride of some rich old man." His eyes lowered to her cleavage. "Throw in a kiss and I'll say I never saw you." He smiled a devilish smile at her and she sneered.

"Get away from me before I make you," she said through gritted teeth. She turned her back on him and he grabbed her wrist, pulling him back to him. As she turned, she raised her arm and slapped him hard across the face. She heard the room gasp.

"Unhand me you fiend!" She screeched, raising her voice several octaves, ensuring that she drew more attention to them. "Just because I am the captain of a ship does not mean I am not a lady, get back!"

She watched as several men came to her aid, taking the man by the arms and hauling him out of the room. A few of the braver ladies around her came forward to guide her to one of the couches that lined the walls, they shoved drinks and sweets at her, asking if she had been harmed in any way and telling her that she had been brave.

All the while her mind was reeling, how could she have let her guard down enough to allow someone onto her ship that was clearly after Zircon? She searched for Topaz, finding him in a corner speaking with a young man; he looked to be about twenty years old, his dark brown hair had also been slicked back and he had a handlebar mustache that was clearly the topic of their conversation. Topaz was twisting the end of his own mustache while the younger gentleman laughed loudly. By the expensive look of his cream colored suit, Mira assumed he was the owner of the house.

Topaz shook hands with the man and turned back to the room, searching for her. When he was in front of her, he took her hand, "Thank you very much for rescuing my companion ladies." He told them, flashing his most dazzling smile, making a few of the women blush.

"You've been very brave, my dear." He told Mira, "Let me escort you beck to the ship where you can lay down and rest." He led her to the door where they immediately heard the room start discussing the events that had just taken place.

"That was a very good distraction," Tope said when they were on the little path from the house again.

"It wasn't a distraction, you idiot. There was a man was sent by Zircon's father, who has apparently now put a price on my head, he told me that if I handed her over willingly that he would tell Mr. Creed that he snatched her from the streets without seeing me." She picked up her speed, needing to check the ship and make sure that Zircon was unharmed.

"Mira, slow down. We need to talk about this. Don't you think it might be time to just give her up? Look at what we've been through this past month. She has brought us nothing but hardship." Mira stopped walking and whirled on him. "You almost died in that storm, Mira. You can't deny that."

"You really know better than to ask me to give up one of my crew. What about the conversation we had an hour ago? You would not make me choose between you, but you would have me give her up at the first sign of trouble?" She was fuming, clenching and unclenching her fists at her sides. She looked down at the ridiculous pink dress she was wearing, it made her feel like a five year old throwing a tantrum and that sent her over the edge. "I'm done with this conversation. Never ask me to abandon anyone again." She turned away from him before he could see the tears forming in her eyes.

"Mira wait, you must see what that woman has done to the crew. To you. You've killed more men in the past month than you ever have before. It cannot sit well with you." Topaz called after but she was too far-gone.

She ran for the docks, away from Topaz and the feelings he was invoking. She couldn't let herself think too hard on the matter without second-guessing herself.

A dark figure stepped out from behind a building, hands in its pockets. Mira stopped and slipped the blade from her sleeve.

"We never got to finish our conversation, Miss Tourmaline," the figure said.

"I have only one thing left to say on the matter." She replied, checking her surroundings for signs of anyone else that might be with him.

He drew his own knife, "And what is that, Miss Tourmaline? You do prefer Miss, correct? Or is it Mister? It is quite confusing with the beard." He let out a low chuckle and stalked forward.

Mira closed her eyes in annoyance, "The only I have to say to is 'duck'."

"Duck?" He asked in confusion.

Before he could take another step, Mira threw her knife at his head. He saw the movement made an attempt to duck but was too slow, the blade struck him in the shoulder.

He let out a cry of pain and pulled the blade free. "Now, now. That wasn't very nice," he gasped.

"I didn't come to play nice," she growled.

She took out a second blade and charged at him. She dropped down to one knee and thrust her knife upward, but he blocked the blow, knocking her forearm away and kicking her in the chest. She fell onto her back and was so surprised that she hesitated a moment too long. He jumped on top of her, his knees pinning her shoulders to the ground. He leaned forward, a knife in each hand and blood in his eyes.

"Care for a shave?" His smile grew wider as he dragged the sharp blade of her own knife down the side of her cheek. She felt the heat of her blood running into her hair, and bared her teeth at him.

Outraged by this, she let out a war cry and bucked, the sudden movement caught him off guard and he rocked backward trying to regain his balance.

Mira took the opportunity to lift her left leg and wrap it around his head, she swiftly pulled it down and he flipped off of her. She scurried backwards and stood, taking the small revolver from her garter and pointing it at his chest. He sat up slowly, a look of pure surprise written across his face.

"How on earth did you do that in a dress?" He demanded. "I must admit that was very impressive."

"Thank you," she said, stalking forward, the barrel of her pistol trained on his chest. "Where is he? When did he send you?"

"Wouldn't you like to know?" He asked her. He touched a hand to his wounded shoulder. "Do you know how much this suit cost?"

"Tell me what I need to know," Mira demanded.

"I'm not telling you anything, freak," he said mockingly. He lifted the dagger at the same time Mira cocked the pistol.

"Wrong choice of words." She said and pulled the trigger.

The look of surprise was still on his face as he fell forward, his blood pooling on the ground around his shoulders.

Mira dropped her arm and took a few unsteady breaths. She closed her eyes as they began to fill again, hearing Topaz's words play over in her mind. He was right; killing so many men did not sit well with her. She saw their deaths play over and over again every time she closed her eyes.

She walked over to the man, wrenched her knife from his hand, and wiped the blood off on his back. Then she set about digging through his trouser pockets, finding nothing of note. She didn't want to flip him over and see his face, so she left him there, facedown in the dirt.

She had just stepped onto the docks when she heard footsteps behind her, and let out a sigh.

"I'm not in the mood for another fight. Say what you have to say so I can go to bed." She said loudly. When she didn't receive a reply she whirled around. "I'm not in the mood Topaz." She stopped short when she saw Emerald standing there, her arms were wrapped around herself and her eyes were wide with fear.

"Emerald," Mira gasped. "What are you doing here? I thought you went back hours ago?"

"I stayed to watch you and Mr. Topaz dance, Miss." The girl said quietly. "I saw that man grab you and followed you to be sure you were safe. I-" Her voice cracked as she let out a sob and fell to her knees. "I was going to run for help but I couldn't move. I couldn't look away in case he killed you."

Mira rushed to her and took her in her arms. "Hush now, it will be alright. There is one less bad man in the world now. It will be alright." Mira started to cry as well, knowing that she was the reason the girl would now be haunted by the sight of the color draining from the man's face, the life leaving his eyes. She closed her own against the images.

They held each other there on the dock until the sun started to rise. Mira looked down to see Emerald fast asleep, tears streaking her dirty face. She stroked the girl's hair, not daring to move lest she wake her.

She heard slow footsteps on the planks behind her and looked over her shoulder, Topaz was walking toward her, his black jacket slung over one shoulder.

"Why don't you hold me like that?" He asked her, a sad smile on his full lips.

"Because you're a great deal bigger." She replied.

He slowly nodded and sat next to her, taking off his boots and placing his long feet into the water. They sat in silence for a moment, him looking out over the ocean and her looking at him.

"You must have killed him quickly," he said quietly.

Mira flinched, "Who?" She asked.

He slowly turned to look at her, his eyes scanning her face. He let out a long breath and shook his head. " I followed you after you ran off. I got a little lost, but I couldn't have been that far behind you. Why not just fight him off? Knock him unconscious and run?"

"Why drag out a fight when I can just kill them and be done with it?" She asked, her voice cold. "I didn't knock him out because he would have just followed us again. Tried to get her again."

He shook his head and sighed.

"Mira, you must admit-"

"I must admit nothing, Topaz. The last time I checked, I was the Captain and you were my first mate, not the other way around."

It was his turn to flinch.

He sucked in a breath and closed his eyes.   "Is that all I am to you now?" He whispered.

"If you continue on this path, yes." She regretted the words as soon as they crossed her lips. He turned his head away from her and she could read the betrayal in the lines of his back.

"If that's how it's to be than." He said as he stood.

"Wait!" Emerald yelled, Mira hadn't realized she was awake and started.

"That was not for your ears, child. Return to the ship. We will be along shortly." Mira told the girl.

"I will not." Emerald said, "I was sent to that house on a mission and I haven't yet showed you what I found." She reached a hand into her pocket and pulled out an enormous diamond ring, a ruby necklace and a hand full of smaller stones.

"Emerald," Topaz breathed, "I told you to only take a few loose stones."

"I thought Miss Peridot would look beautiful in the necklace, and I was planning on giving you the ring to give to Miss Mira." She said with a look full of expectation.

"How very thoughtful," he told her, "I'm sure Miss Peridot will love the necklace. Why don't we go and give it to her. I'll take the gems."

"What about the ring?" She asked, looking between the two of them

"You keep it." He told Emerald gently, "Miss Mira isn't the type to wear such things." Then he took the girl's hand and guided her back to the ship.

Ten

After the ship was repaired
enough to sail without the risk of sinking,
they sailed peacefully for another month,
only stopping in a small fishing port long
enough to resupply their food and
drinking water. Mira was so suddenly
thrown back into her childhood at the
sight of it, that she chose not to leave the
ship, sending the rest of the crew out to
stretch their legs.

Once they were back on the water,
it was clear that the crew was getting
restless from so many days spent out at
sea without performing. So Mira hatched
a plan, they would put on a show for
themselves. They were all given three
days notice so they could shake out the
rust of being still for so long.

An hour before the performances were to start, there was a knock at Mira's door.

"Come." She called. She was attempting to find a shirt that didn't have any tears. When the door remained shut, she called out again, louder this time. "Come in!" Still, no one came in.

She strode across the room and flung the door open, ready to bite someone's head off, but no one was there. She looked down the passageway but didn't see anyone. She was about to shut the door when she noticed a small bundle folded nicely on the floor. She looked over the passageway again but saw no one, so she picked it up and brought it inside.

She unfolded the thing to find that it was one of her better dresses; she whirled around to see that it was indeed missing from its hook near her bunk. She held it up to the light to reveal fine lace had been sewn around the bodice and waist, and tiny rhinestones had been added across the entire thing, they sparkled in the light as she turned it this way and that.

"What in the world?" She muttered.

There was a note pinned to a shoulder that read, "Wear me" in neat script.

"Pearl." Mira said, letting out a low chuckle.

"Put it on!" Emerald shouted from behind her. Mira turned to see the girl standing in her doorway. One of her dresses had also been altered, the once sack like material was now cinched just below the chest with a white ribbon that was tied in a princess knot in the back, the once long sleeves had been cut short and matching cuffs and collar had been added. Emerald herself had obviously been washed, and her hair was plaited in two pigtails tied at the ends with more white ribbons. The grin she wore was contagious.

"Well now, look at you!" Mira said letting out a whistle. "Give us a twirl."

Emerald did so with such enthusiasm that she almost fell over, Mira laughed and clapped. "You look like the belle of the ball, Emerald dear."

"Thank you, Miss. I helped Miss Pearl gather the materials when we last made port. She fixed up an outfit for everyone!" The girl told her.

"That was very kind of you two," Mira said. "Come now, help me get into this contraption." They laughed as they worked together to lace up the back of Mira's dress. Emerald pulled out a matching piece of lace ribbon from her pocket and used it to tie back Mira's long locks.

When they made there way to the deck, they saw that the lanterns were lit and a giant pile of throw rugs, blankets, and pillows had been stacked against the helm. Spinel was sitting on a water barrel near them, playing her guitar. The skirt she wore had been remade to look like the sun. Pearl had taken the dark yellow material and added lighter shades throughout, over the top of this was a sheer material with glittery rhinestones attached. The stays she wore were also made of a dark shade of yellow silk. She shone as she moved, making it look as if the sun itself was turning in the sky, the effect was mesmerizing.

The twins appeared next; they were dressed as opposites tonight, not twins as they usually were. Aventurine was dressed as she usually was, in white, but her body suit was now skintight, showing off her lean muscular form, with long lace attached to the straps, making it look as if she had wings sprouting from her back. Mira would have thought she was naked if it weren't for the black "A" stitched into the left side of her chest; she wore a sour expression.

Citrine on the other hand, was wrapped in black material. His costume had also been made to hug his form, making the distinctions between brother and sister more prominent. He had a white "C" stitched upon a shoulder, and a short cape of black silk attached to his shoulders. He beamed with pride as he walked to the main mast and began his stretches.

Peridot was shuffling her cards at a table, a large blanket wrapped around her. Emerald must have seen the look on Mira's face, she cleared her throat and said, "Miss Peridot was given a brand-new gown since none of hers fit anymore, she will reveal it during her performance." She explained.

Mira felt a sting in her heart at that. She hadn't bought Peridot new material for dresses as a way to try and get her off of the ship, but maybe that had been the wrong thing to do. She could see

Peridot chewing nervously at her lower lip and hoped it wasn't because of her.

"And where is Miss Pearl?" Mira asked the girl.

"She's below deck warming up, Miss, warming up," Emerald said.

"Warming up?" Mira asked curiously.

"Yes Miss, for her performance." With that Emerald was off, jumping up into the arms of Citrine who twirled her around as they both laughed.

Mira looked around at her ship, she couldn't remember the last time she felt so content, happy almost, but there was something nagging at the back of her mind. She rubbed the spot, trying to dislodge the feeling. A hand caught her wrist and held it above her head, and she spun around.

"Do that again, but slower." Topaz told her, his voice low in a way that made her skin come alive.

She did as he asked, spinning slower this time and relishing the way his eyes raked over her.

"I think I might be starting to like Pearl," he told her, sweeping his eyes up and down her body again. She hadn't realized until now that her bodice had also been cut about an inch lower.

"Don't make me blush in front of the men," she told him playfully.

He grabbed her waist and pulled her close, she tipped her head back and eyed his lips.

"I wouldn't dream of it," he told her as he leaned in and kissed her gently.

Someone gave a whoop and Mira tried to pull away, laughing with embarrassment. Topaz clutched her tighter and rested his forehead on hers. Spinel started playing her guitar again and Peridot joined in with her flute. Topaz started swaying them gently back and forth in time with the music. Emerald started to sing in an enchanting soprano about a lonely mermaid looking for her sailor boy, surprising everyone. Mira closed her eyes and moved to put her head on Topaz's shoulder, he pulled her closer and she felt him relax.

"You look absolutely delicious in that dress," he murmured in her ear.

"Don't ruin the moment," she told him and felt him chuckle beneath her cheek.

When the singing ended, he held her for a moment longer, when they looked around they saw the crew watching them with smiles on every face.

Mira blushed and was about to speak when she saw Zircon, her arms were crossed tightly across her chest and she was trying not to look at the couple.

Mira cleared her throat. "Right than, lets get this started! Who wants to go first?"

It was a night fit for royalty. Everyone had gone through the trouble of learning some new trick and showing off their great skills. They clapped and laughed as each performance ended, showing great enthusiasm for every twist and turn. Aventurine had gone to great lengths to make as much of a feast for them that she could manage with her meager kitchen. There were grilled fish, rolls, three different types of potatoes and most shockingly, a roasted duck. There were casks of wine and port. Everyone thanked Aventurine wholeheartedly.

"There won't be much of him for everyone," Aventurine said, pointing to the duck. "But we can all pretend to be civilized people for the night and take small portions like they do at fancy dinners." They all laughed.

Everyone was a star that night, but Mira's eyes kept drifting back to Zircon. She had barely noticed the twins flipping and spinning through the air; they had trained themselves to fly in ways that Mira never thought humanly possible. They all held their breath as Aventurine stretched out her long limbs to reach for her swing as she flew out of her brother's grasp. Aventurine looked like an angel flying through the night, come to save them all. Citrine looked like Death chasing her, Mira shuttered at the sight.

Zircon had captured her attention from the moment she stepped before them. She had asked Spinel to play a jig on her guitar, which she had surprisingly agreed to. She had spun, kicked, and twirled her way across Mira's heart. Mira had thought she would try her hand at singing, like she said she was going to, but when asked, she replied that she had tried her best but Emerald told her she should stick to dancing.

When she was finished, the crew had clapped, but not as loudly, and Mira could see the discomfort on Zircon's face. She spent the next performance trying to catch the woman's eye, but Zircon just stared straight ahead.

Peridot stepped up next, fidgeting and clearly nervous.

"Go on, Per." Mira said encouragingly. "We're all excited to see what you have in store for us."

Peridot dropped down to the floor and began to shuffle her oldest tarot deck, the ones her mother had given her and that she reserved for special readings. She began to read what she referred to as the ocean's cards, but Mira thought they were more likely hers.

Topaz could tell she was uncomfortable so he began to slowly run his thumb up and down her arm. The sensation was so soothing that she leaned into him. He took the opportunity to drape an arm around her and pointedly looked down her dress. They were playfully nudging each other when Peridot suddenly rose to her feet.

"So says the cards." She said loudly, throwing off the blanket that had been draped around her to reveal a silk gown made of the most stunning shade of cerulean Mira had ever seen. They all clapped for Peridot and her cheeks pinked, she bent down to collect the cards scattered around her feet.

"You look amazing Per," Mira said to her.

She got a mumbled thank you in reply and nothing else. Clearly Peridot was upset about just now having a new gown after so many years aboard the ship. Mira made a mental note to apologize to her tomorrow.

"Well then, I guess that's our cue," Topaz said as he stood. "Has anyone seen dear Amethyst?" He asked, hands clasped behind his back and a smirk on his lips.

Everyone sat up, looking around and started to shake their heads.

"Hmm, well I guess I'll have to wait until she arrives." Tope started to slowly pace back and forth in front of the crowd. The crew started to grow restless, looking around and talking quietly with one another.

"Quiet now," Topaz said with a finger to his lips, " I hear her now."

The crowd hushed, straining his or her ears to listen for the giant snake. Emerald began to whimper and Peridot wrapped an arm tightly around her.

Citrine sat up, "I'm not sure she's here Tope, perhaps she's in your bunk still?"

"Oh she's here alright." Topaz said ghoulishly. His eyes swept up and a slow smile crept to his lips.

All heads snapped up to see Amethyst directly above them. She was wrapped around a loose rope, slowly inching her way toward them, her long tongue flicking just inches above their heads. Emerald and Peridot let out startled squeals at the same time and then began to giggle nervously.

Amethyst had stopped her slow decent when they looked up at her, her head slowly swung back and forth, looking at each of them in turn. She began to inch forward again in the direction of Emerald.

"Amethyst," Topaz said in a haunting voice. "Eat."

She lunged forward, landing at Emerald's feet and let out a loud hiss. Emerald screamed in terror and jumped high into the air, then scrambled to Mira and buried her face in her skirts. Amethyst watched all of this happen out of one serpentine eye, let out another hissed and slithered to Topaz. She crawled up his long legs and wound her way around his arms and neck. When she was in place, Topaz gave a deep bow. No one clapped.

Do you intend to scare off all of the patrons with that act?" Aventurine asked.

Topaz said nothing, just smirked and took his place beside Mira.

"You know that's how I've trained Tanz to eat his fish." Spinel said to him. "You stole that trick from me."

"I did, but how much more terrifying is it when it's an eight foot snake?" He asked. No one replied. "Besides, you would never do that in a show, would you?"

Spinel sat back and crossed her arms. Mira could hear her mumbling something but couldn't make out much more than "Pilfering bastard." She let out a chuckle and took a deep drink of her wine.

Pearl stepped in front of them, they all whispered to each other. Pearl had been extremely secret about what her talent would be, she told no one but Citrine and he had been sworn to secrecy. He had been spotted in the days before their performances, gathering large pieces of wood from wherever they could be found. Pearl would disappear into her cabin for hours at a time, not a sound could be heard from the other side of the door, so everyone assumed she was stitching something together.

Citrine brought out a large board, about seven feet tall and four feet wide, and stood in front of it with his hands behind his back. Pearl smiled a devilish smile at the small crowd. She wore a floor length cape that she threw off with a flourish. Beneath it she had on a simple gown made of purple cotton, nothing noteworthy other that its simplicity. It was what was around her waist that drew the crew's eyes.

She wore a leather belt with a row of small daggers, sharp as fresh quills, tucked all the way around her slim waist. Mira sat a little straighter, but Citrine gave her a small nod, then turned his attention back to Pearl. She gave a small bow, turned to Citrine with fierce concentration and loosed a dagger.

Aventurine shot to her feet and was about to lunge forward when Spinel grabbed her ankle.

"Look," she whispered.

The dagger stuck into the board just above Citrine's head. His eyes were closed. Pearl took a visible breath and loosed two more. They landed on either side of his face. The crew watched in silent horror as this went on for ten more throws.

When she was done, Pearl turned to them and gave another silent bow. As she straightened Mira could see a look of uncertainty in her eyes as they flicked toward Aventurine. Everyone was silent.

"Ships and Seas." Peridot said quietly.

They all clamped thunderously after that, Citrine's face started to glow with pride. He walked over to Pearl, drew her close to his side and kissed her cheek. They were all so shocked by this obvious sign of affection from him that they stopped clapping.

"Well then." Spinel said, "I guess that leaves us." She called Tanzanite over to her and they went in front of the crowd. Mira was so distracted by Aventurine's quiet, furious whispers toward her brother that she hardly paid attention and was startled when Emerald jumped up from her seat next to her and clapped so loudly it hurt Mira's ears.

"That was marvelous! Absolutely wonderful!" She had obviously been picking up on Pearl's way of speaking, "How ever did you teach a lion to dance?" The younger girl asked.

Spinel had always had a deep connection with Tanz, he lived off of fish that she would catch for him and only listened to her. He was very much like an overgrown sheep dog; able to learn just about anything she could teach him in a matter of days.

"All you have to do is ask nicely and he will do whatever trick you teach him, much like you and that chew toy." Spinel said with a mischievous smile, inclining her said to Emerald's bird.

Emerald stood and put her arm out for the bird. "Right then, let's show them what we've got up our sleeve!" She told the creature.

"Dar she blows! Abandon ship!" It replied.

"Please tell me she's taught it something new to say." Mira mumbled to Topaz. He laughed and patted her hand.

Emerald gave a bow, extending her arms out to the sides, the little parrot hopped down into one outstretched hand and then the other. In unison, they bowed their heads, then stood straight and stuck out a foot.

"Well now! Look at this!" Topaz cheered. "Well done Emerald, I thought that bird was good for nothing but giving Miss Mira a headache!"

Emerald glared at him and stood. "That's not the best part," she said, looking down her nose at him. The bird flew to perch atop her head and said, "Miss Mira, Miss Mira."

Everyone looked from the bird to Mira. They were quiet for several seconds before they all burst out laughing.

"How wonderful," Mira said into her cup.

Emerald's face fell, "Do you not like it Miss?" She asked.

"I love it Emerald. Very good job, it will be a great addition to your show when we get to port." Mira told her.

Everyone went silent again.

"We're making port?" Emerald asked, "To perform?"

"Yes." Mira said, "I think it's time we show ourselves off again. I never thought I'd say it, but I think I'm beginning to get a little sea sick, being out here for so long." She laughed but no one joined her, they were all looking at Topaz.

"Right, I think we could all use a good night's rest then." he said, "Well done everyone, very good job."

"But Mr. Topaz hasn't performed for us yet." Emerald pouted.

"I perform for you all everyday, little one. Go on. Everyone to their bunks," Topaz said with more force than was necessary.

The rest of the crew slowly made their way to their own corners of the ship, leaving Mira and Topaz sitting on the pile of blankets that had been left behind.

"When did you decide this?" He asked her. He was laying back and looking up at the stars.

"Just now," Mira said.

"Are you going to give her up?" Topaz asked quietly.

Mira closed her eyes and stood, walked to her bunk, and closed the door.

The next morning, Mira brought her maps to Peridot's cabin. She knocked several times before finally opening the door. The room was empty.

"Strange," Mira thought.

She made her way to the helm and tried to map out their best course on her own. She was still there cursing the thing when Topaz came up the steps. Mira could tell he was up to something by the way he crossed his arms as he approached.

"What?" she said to him, not looking up.

"We need to talk Mira." He told her, his voice was firm, not at all like the quiet tone he usually reserved for her.

"Talk then," she replied, trying to hide her anxiousness.

"Mira, you know how the crew feels. This has gone on long enough. It's time to let her go. There is no telling what her devil of a father will do to us if he finds us now." He stood next to her, looking down at the maps.

"Let's make port here," he said after a moment, pointing to a spot of the map. "It's a small enough town, we can dump her there in the middle of the night and run. They won't give chase forever, especially not if they have her. We will have to lay low for a while, maybe even do some trading, but we will manage." He took her hand and turned her so they were facing. "Please, Mira, do this for us."

The way he said it made Mira's eyes well up, her head told her that he meant the crew, but her heart knew better. She had not allowed him into her bunk for quite some time; the late night rendezvous had ended shortly after Zircon had arrived and made her way into Mira's every thought. He was tearing her apart each time he asked her to turn Zircon away.

"Topaz," she began, but stopped when she couldn't form the words, gesturing around wildly.

"I thought I would give it one last try." He walked away from her then, and Mira got the feeling that he was walking away from much more than their conversation.

Eleven

They docked two days later, in a decent sized port that was known for its enormous wildflower fields and honeysuckle wine. The crew set off as soon as the ship was tied off, even Peridot went, much to everyone's surprise. She was wearing the dress that Pearl had made for her, when Mira raised a shocked brow at her she said:"It would be a shame if no one saw it."

Topaz had hefted Emerald onto his broad shoulders and told her they needed to find something sweet to eat. Pearl had her arm tucked into the crook of Citrine's arm, her parasol draped over her shoulder. Aventurine had her arm locked with Peridot's, a sour expression on her face, and Spinel took her usual place at the back, always looking out for trouble.

Mira hung back with the excuse that someone needed to stay with the ship now that Peridot was gone, but she really wanted to speak with Zircon, who hadn't come above deck yet.

"Captain," she heard as she was scrubbing the railing that Tanzanite had been rubbing his dirty side into. "I can get that, you should go ashore. You must be tired of being on this boat."

She turned to see Zircon standing near her; she wore a sailor's costume, not her usual dress.

"What are you wearing?" Mira asked her without thinking.

Zircon's cheeks flared lightly pink. "I thought I would draw less attention if I dressed like a man, like you did when you came for me."

Mira laughed, "I draw less attention when I'm dressed as a man because it's harder to tell that I am a woman." She said with a pointed look at Zircon's chest.   Zircon stuffed her hands into her armpits and turned red.

"Those are not the only curves you have, Love." The word slipped out before she knew what she was saying. They both froze and Mira looked down at the brush in her hand, she couldn't help but think back to the day she woke after the storm and had held those curves close to hers.

"I would like a word with you, if you aren't too busy," Zircon told her quietly.

Mira dropped the brush into the bucket and stood, keeping her eyes averted. Zircon was quiet for several moments.

"I do not wish to leave you." Mira's head snapped up at this. "The crew, I mean," Zircon said quickly, "The ship. I know they don't like me, and they think I am more trouble than I am worth. But I cannot go back to the life I lived. I would rather die." There was a strong defiance in her eyes as she said this. "I am not being dramatic Mira; I wouldn't survive if I were forced to live with my father ever again. You wouldn't believe the things he made me do, the things he himself has done to me. I will hurl myself off this ship into the jaws of a shark before I go back to him. I won't do it." She was crying now, great heaving sobs that wracked her entire body. "I can't."

Before she could stop herself, Mira went to her and wrapped her arms around her waist, pulling her in tight. She stroked her hair and said soothing things into her ear.

"It's alright, I won't make you return to him. I won't abandon you, I swear it." Mira took her face in hers and made Zircon look her in the eye. "I will hear no more of this," She told her fiercely.

"If they come for me again Mira, I want you to kill me. Shoot me dead where I stand, so I will not have to live a life like that ever again. Kill me Mira, please." Zircon begged.

Mira pushed her lips to Zircon's in hopes that it would silence the horrible words that were coming out of her lovely mouth. She meant to stop after just one, but Zircon pulled her so desperately back to her that Mira lost control. She pulled her waist to her and they groped at each other with all of their might, their kisses turning hungrier and hungrier with each passing second. Mira swore she could feel her heart growing, reaching out with all of its might to reach into Zircon's chest and heal her every wound. She wanted so fiercely to help her that she couldn't stop herself from what she was doing.

Zircon's fingertips were sliding into the seam of Mira's breeches when someone cleared their throat. They wretched apart to see Spinel standing at the gangway, her cheeks were flushed and she looked thoroughly embarrassed. Mira looked down and realized that she had Zircon propped up against the railing and her legs were wrapped tightly about her waist and Mira's shirt was open much farther than it had been before.

"Aventurine has decided to leave. I thought I would come to warn you before the others get here." Spinel said. "They aren't happy Mira." She gave Zircon a pointed look.

Mira dropped Zircon. "What do you mean leave? Leave the crew?" She asked.

"I'll let her tell you." Spinel told her, then turned and headed back down the gangway toward town.

"I'm sorry," Mira told Zircon, for what, she didn't know.

She looked over to see the woman with a hand to her swollen lips, her checks were flushed and her hair was a mess. When Zircon didn't reply, Mira turned to walk away. She was almost to the helm when Zircon spoke.

"I never meant for this to happen."
Mira slowed and listened. "Promise me,
Mira. Promise me that you will kill me
when they come for me," she said.

Mira stopped in her tracks her
own fingertips touching her lips. She
closed her eyes.

"I will do no such thing." She said
over her shoulder.

Mira was waiting for them at the
main mast when the crew finally arrived.
She had calmed down somewhat and
splashed herself with cold water to get rid
of her nerves. She knew that whatever
was coming wouldn't be good.

Topaz was at the head of the
group, his face flushed with anger.
Emerald held his hand and hurried to
keep up with his angry steps. The others
followed slowly behind; their faces were a
range of emotions. Mira had to steel
herself against her oncoming tears.

"This is all your doing," Pearl
stormed as she came aboard. Citrine and
Aventurine were behind her, hand in
hand, and both had red-rimmed eyes.

Mira said nothing.

"I wish to leave The Oddity's
Revenge." Aventurine said loudly, she

thrust a missing person's poster into Mira's chest. At the bottom was a description of the ship and Mira, asking that she be detained for questioning.

"The time has come, enough is enough. I will not risk my life for that woman any longer. I encourage the rest of you to do the same," Aventurine told them.

No one spoke a word, they scarcely risked breathing. Mira's heart hammered in her chest.

"If that is what you wish, I won't stop you," she said.

Everyone brow rose at her. Citrine's jaw fell open.

"You can't be serious," he said, when it was obvious that she was, he went on. "Mira, for the love of the sea, please come to your senses. This is madness! Are you actually telling us that you would rather have her as a part of your crew than my sister? We have sailed with you for eight years. You know us. We know you. You know nothing of that woman other than she has a beautiful face." He was crying now, Mira had never seen him cry before.

She stayed silent.

"It is just as I thought Brother, she would rather have that harlot on her ship than me. That is fine. I have never been very fond of Miss Mira Tourmaline or this ship. I will gather my things and leave." Aventurine strode past them, head held high. They all stood in stunned silence, waiting for Mira to speak.

"You cannot ask me to give up one of my crew." She told them darkly. "I will not. If I gave up one I would be forced to give you all up," she turned her back and faced the sea. "This has never been a prison for any of you. I have never and will never force you to do anything against your will." She turned back to them with tears in her eyes.

"This ship was given to me by a great man who took me in as his own, when my own mother couldn't bare the sight of me. I took it as my sign to do the same thing with more people like me." She looked at each of them in turn. Holding the gaze of whoever would meet her eye. "Leave if you must. Stay if you will."

She turned back towards the sea and let her tears fall of their own accord, she could hear muffled conversation behind her but not much else.

Aventurine came up a short while later, a small sack over her shoulder. "I wish you luck brother. May we meet again one day." With that, she strode off the ship and was gone.

Mira turned back to the crew and was slapped. Her head whirled to the side and she ducked down on instinct, hand going to her dagger. She looked up to see Peridot standing above her, her fists balled at her sides, she was crying.

"How dare you," she whispered.

Mira was shocked; none of her crew had ever dared to raise a hand at her before. She brought a hand to her cheek and looked to the rest of the crew.

"How dare you, indeed." Spinel said.

They all turned as a group, and left her standing by herself, clutching the railing for support. She let out a frustrated yell and followed them below deck.

"We will stay in port as long as it takes to win Aventurine back. I will not leave this place without her," she called after them.

None of them responded, they continued walking away to their cabins.

"I will get her back." She said quietly.

In the end, they waited three days before the first wanted poster went up. It showed a picture of Mira, her beard was slightly longer and her features more masculine than they were in person, but there was no denying it was her. The next day, Topaz's poster went up. That same afternoon, it was the twins. By the end of the week, the entire crew had wanted posters up and down the docks and all over the local taverns, even little Emerald with her bird perched on her shoulder.

They all said the same thing:

WANTED FOR KIDNAPPING AND MURDER

Zircon's poster was different than the rest. Her picture was a perfect likeness and even sported the neckline of her gown to show her three breasts. Below this, the poster read:

MISSING AND ENDANGERED PLEASE HELP US BRING A BELOVED DAUGHTER HOME

The crew was enraged with Mira and Zircon and terrified that the town would turn them over.

Citrine and Pearl refused to leave without Aventurine, so Mira was forced to stay along with them, or risk losing the entire crew. No one spoke as they moved about their daily tasks; it was as if ghosts were managing the ship.

On the morning of the seventh day, Emerald came up the gangway, looking over her shoulder as if being chased. Mira watched as she spoke to Topaz. His posture went ridged and he turned his sharp eyes to Mira, it was the first time he had looked at her since Aventurine left.

He stormed over to where she was repairing a board on the deck.

"There is a swarm of men in the village. They're spreading word that they mean to take Zircon and kill the rest of us if necessary," he boomed.

Mira looked down at the board she was working on.

"Very well," she whispered.

Twelve

Mira woke to a small hand shaking her arm. She peeled open an eye and saw Emerald's face mere inches from her own; she looked terrified.

"What is it?" Mira asked, shooting up in bed, pistol already in her hand.

"The men Miss, they're here," Emerald replied.

"No," Mira breathed. She set about the cabin, collecting weapons and tugging on her boots.

"Where?" She asked, searching her desk for spare knives.

"They posted a wanted poster on the ship, Miss. Right near the gangway. There are three men at the end of the dock keeping watch over the ship,"

Emerald replied, she had begun to hop from foot to foot.

Mira crossed the room and kneeled down, pushing something into the girl's small hands.

"Run, take that rotten bird of yours and go. I met with the fish merchant's wife yesterday, she said you could stay with them until you're able to stay on your own." Mira wiped a tear that escaped from the corner of the girl's eye.

"None of that, we don't have time for it. Take the rope ladder at the back of the ship and swim to shore. They won't see you if you're careful," she turned the girl around and gave her a small push toward the door.

Emerald rushed from the room, holding her arm over her eyes so Mira wouldn't see her cry.

After she was gone, Mira counted to fifty and then crept from the room. She kept low against the railing, occasionally peaking over to search for the men Emerald had mentioned. When she reached the hold, she quickened her steps to Topaz's cabin.

"Get up. They're here." She quietly called through the crew's doors as she went.

Spinel was the first to open her door, already dressed for a fight. She wore her finest skirt and stays, with every gun she owned strapped at her waist and sides. She gave Mira a nod and headed for the steps.

"There are three at the end of the dock," Mira called to her.

"Not for long," Spinel replied.

Mira opened Topaz's door to find him pulling on his breeches, a solemn look on his face. She quietly watched him gather his weapons.

"We knew this would happen eventually," she told him after it was obvious that he was waiting for her.

"Yes, we did. We've all been warning you against this and telling you that we needed to return her to her father since the moment you killed the first group of men." He told her, his voice cold.

"Would you have me return everyone, Tope? Everyone has a family that is looking for them, everyone has a their own reasons to run. No one deserves to live a life locked away, no one deserves to live a life that someone else has chosen for them just because they don't look like 'normal people'." She said to him.

"You and I don't, we could leave before they get here." He replied quietly.

"What would you have me do, Topaz? Abandon the ship and crew and run off into the sunset with you?" She asked, exasperated.

"Yes," he replied simply, "I would. The crew can make their own way. They have plenty of skills other than sailing and performing. You don't have to take care of them forever, Mira." He walked slowly up to her and cupped her cheek.

"We don't have time for this." Mira turned to leave; she didn't want him to see the tears in her eyes.

Topaz turned back to his bunk, where Amethyst lay coiled.

"Keep the bunk safe, Amethyst. If they come aboard, hide the good gin." He told his pet, then gave her a small salute and closed the door. He rested his hand on the wood for a moment turning to go.

The rest of the crew was already waiting when they reached the deck. They were crouched near the gangway, stealing looks down the dock at the men.

"Citrine, get to the crow's nest and give us a proper view," Mira instructed.

As he crept along the deck, Mira turned back to the others.

"Right. We knew this day was coming, it was only a matter of time before they caught up to us," she told them, Spinel was the only one that would look her in the eye, so she focused on her. "I understand if you want to leave, you've all made it very clear how you feel about this situation." She looked to Zircon, who only stared at the deck; her heart sank. "I would do the same thing for any of you, you all know that. I would fight and kill for reach and every one of you. Will you do the same for me?" She lifted her chin a fraction and stared them down, hoping against hope that they would join her.

To her surprise, Pearl was the first to speak, raising her large hand to her pistol.

"Aye, Captain," she said, just loud enough to hear. There was a new spark in her eyes that Mira could have sworn were tears. "I will fight for these people, our people."

Unsurprisingly, Citrine was next. He stood next to Pearl and clutched her hand, nodding his head once to Mira.

"Aye, Captain," Spinel told her quietly.

She then looked back over Citrine's shoulder and held her hand out to

Peridot, who closed her eyes in defeat and stepped forward, reaching to clutch Spinel's hand.

"We never did know when to quit," she told Mira.

Mira gave her a nod of her head, than turned to the rest, they all gave her a nod and they set about their plan. She went to the wheel and inch-by-inch turned the helm so the sails were facing against the wind. She felt a sting in her eyes as she watched the rest of the crew hurry about, crouched low to the floor to avoid being seen by the men down the dock.

She was dabbing her eyes with a spare bandana when Citrine soundlessly dropped to the deck next to her.

"There is a ship anchored about two miles out, Cap. It's flying the crown's colors." He had a worried look in his eye and he had begun to sweat despite the early morning chill.

"Very well," she said quietly.

He stayed near her, seemingly wanting to say something but thought better of it and left to find Pearl.

Mira took a deep breath and steadied herself as they began to very slowly make their way out to sea. She planned to stay close to the shoreline; going out only as far as was necessary. She kept one eye trained on the enemy ship, and one on Zircon. The rest of the crew was keeping a wide berth, and she kept her head down, winding the anchor rope up and out of the way.

She closed her eyes against it all, she hoped that they would one day understand the love she had for each of them, the feeling she got when they rescued another helpless person from living a life they didn't want.

Topaz came slowly toward her, his arms crossed and head down. "Throw her overboard Mira. Toss her out and we will run. They shouldn't give chase if they have her."

"I will not. We have never backed down from a fight, we can still get away-"

"For how long Mira?" His voice was dangerously quiet. "How long will you have us run for?"

"As long as it takes. They will give up eventually," she knew that this was unlikely, but she had to try.

As if knowing her thoughts, he asked her, "Would you give up the rest of us for her Mira? Someone is eventually going to get hurt, or worse. You will have to choose between us soon enough. You have already lost one of us to her, you must know the rest of us are not far behind." He turned his back to her and let the words hang there between them.

"So be it," she said, her voice thick with the tears that ran freely down her cheeks. "This is a sanctuary, a safe place. It has never been a cage. They are free to go if they so wish, I will not be their keeper."

"And what about me?" He asked, looking in her direction over his shoulder. "Are you no longer my keeper?"

"I will be whatever you wish me to be, for as long as you wish me to be it." She left the helm and stood behind him. "But you cannot ask this of me." She reached a hand out to his shoulder, but he saw the movement and stepped away. When his head disappeared below deck, she fell to the deck and let out a great sob. She could feel herself losing this battle and she couldn't bare it.

Just then a loud shout came from above, "Mira! She is after us!"

Mira jerked her head up to see Citrine, standing on the main sail pointing behind them. She rushed to the railing to see the great ship coming toward them quickly.

"Shit," she breathed, why had she thought they would just let them go?

"Drop sails!" She bellowed, turning back to the helm, giving it a great pull until they were heading to open sea.

"We will never make it!" Peridot yelled. "Mira, go back to port! We will give her to them and be done with this! Please!" She ran to Mira, grabbing the front of her shirt in desperation. "Please Mira, they will kill us all."

"I cannot give up one of my crew." She told the crying woman, "I would not turn over any of you, you know this!"

"No one else poses the threat that she does! No one of worth is looking for any of us! No one is looking for any of us anymore! Give her back, Mira!"

Mira pushed her friend away and she stumbled to the deck, giving a cry of alarm. Peridot looked up at Mira with tear filled eyes. "She will be the death of him," she said, reminding Mira of the vision she had about Topaz and Zircon.

"Not now, Per. We must get away before they are too close to us," she snapped.

Mira looked up to see that the sails were still wrapped firmly around the main mast.

"Citrine!" She bellowed again. "Why are the sails still secured?" She looked around for him but could only see Pearl standing in the middle of the deck. Her arms were crossed and she was glaring up at Mira.

"We will not run." Pearl said, her voice set with grim determination. "You will not make us."

Mira stared in surprise. "Where is Citrine?"

"I told him to go below deck with the others." Pearl said in the same cool voice.

"You what?" Mira boomed, coming to stand in front of Pearl. "This is *my* ship! How dare you tell my crew what to do?"

"How dare you ask them to risk their lives for such a lost cause?" Pearl asked, voice low. "We were willing to fight off a few men, but a royal ship? You ask too much Mira, we are choosing to live."

Mira ran to the railing to check the progress of the ship, it was getting closer by the second.

"As I said, they are all below deck. Maybe you should come down and finally listen to what they have to say." With that, Pearl turned and left Mira standing alone in the middle of the deck. With no other choice, Mira followed her down the steep steps, knowing what must be done now.

They were gathered in the galley, and silent as the grave when Mira ducked below the low door and entered. She looked around the room, all of them, except Zircon who she couldn't see, were staring straight at her.

"Out with it then," she demanded.

They all looked at each other, seemingly trying to decide who would voice their opinions for them. In the end, it was Spinel.

"We can't win this fight, Mira," she said. There was no fight in her voice, just calm resolve. "We must turn her over. Enough is enough."

"Is that what you all want?" She asked, voice low.

They all stared at her. They had made it very clear for some time now that this is what they wanted still, she had to be sure.

"What does she have to say about all of this? Where is she?" She asked of Zircon.

"She is in her bunk," This came from Pearl, "collecting her things."

They were all quiet, no one daring to say the thing that they were all thinking. That they blamed Mira for the hell that was about to be brought down upon them now that the crown was involved.

"If this is what you have chosen, then you must hear what I have chose," Mira began, "I will take Zir- Elizabeth," She corrected, now that she was no longer a part of the crew, there was no point in calling her by the name. "Above deck. You lot will stay here and wait for us to be taken by whatever devil has come to collect us. I will tell them that I have acted alone and forced you all to play along with this mad plan. Which is the truth, is it not?" No one spoke a word. She cleared her throat and continued on, "Once we are gone Topaz will take over the ship with Peridot as his first mate." Peridot's head snapped up at this. "The papers have already been drawn up, they are in the some drawer in my desk, I'm sure you will be able to find them. Then you will sail away from here and never look back, and you will never return." She told them.

"So you are choosing her over us once more?" Peridot demanded, more of a statement than a question.

"I am choosing to set you free of the burden I created and pay for my mistakes," Mira told them all. "I would die for each and every one of you, the least you can do is live for me."

They all stared at her in different fazes of shock.

Elizabeth, for she was Elizabeth now, came in behind Mira. She wore the same dress and ridiculous hat that she had worn on the first day she came to the ship, and carried her overstuffed bag in both hands. Mira's heart thundered at the sight of her tear-streaked face, she clearly didn't want to return to her father, but she was unwilling to let the rest of them suffer for her any longer.

"I am ready to face them Mira." Elizabeth said quietly, looking at the floor. "You may throw me overboard if you wish, I only ask that you give me a bit of rope to tie my bag about myself first."

"No one is going overboard," Mira started, but a loud boom drowned out the rest of her words. The sound of splintering wood made them all jump to their feet.

"No!" Mira cried, rushing for the stairs. The crew followed close behind her crying out as another loud crash sounded overhead.

"Everyone stay low! They are firing their cannons at us!" Mira bellowed as she reached the deck. She withdrew one of her pistols and checked its primer, pulled the hammer back and fired once up into the air. She then tore the bottom half of her shirt off, jumped onto the railing and waved it wildly above her head, attempting to signal her surrender.

She felt the shot before she heard it. A bullet tore through her left shoulder and she flew backwards, slamming into the deck.

"Mira!" Topaz screamed. He charged forward with all the force of a bull, flinging himself on top of her to protect her from any other attacks.

"Get off," she grunted. "Your weight is worse than the bullet."

He clutched her face, "What in the name of the seven seas were you thinking?" He demanded, ripping his shirt over his head and pressing it into her wounded shoulder.

She looked down at his bare chest. "What is it with us and our shirts?" She asked him.

His attention was on the other ship, "They're preparing to board us," he told her.

"Dar she blows! Abandon ship!" Mira heard a voice screech.

"Help me up, I mean to face them on my feet," she told Topaz.

She reached her feet just as the first sailor dropped from a rope swing. He took a knife from between his rotten teeth and looked to Mira with a bloodthirsty grin.

"Well, hello there Captain," he said in a mocking tone.

"Get off my ship," she told him between her teeth.

He barked out a laugh and approached her, "Or what? I didn't believe the boss when he told us we were after a lady with a beard, but I didn't believe it was true! Look at you! What a freak!"

"Bad choice of words, friend." Topaz called as Mira let out a growl. "We don't use that word on this ship."

"And what are you supposed to be? A lion?" The intruder called to Topaz.

"No," called a female voice, "*This* is the lion. Tanz, eat."

Tanzanite charged from the shadows at the intruder, releasing a roar just before pouncing and ripping his throat out. Another sailor from the other boat had landed on the railing and watched this in horror; he let out a string of curses as he swung back to his ship.

"Where is she?" Mira boomed, looking around for Elizabeth.

Spinel ran to her, pointedly not looking at Tanzanite as he continued with his meal. "They won't let us go now, not after that." She yelled.

"Damn them all to the bottom of the sea!" Citrine yelled. He had one arm wrapped tightly around Pearl's waist. She was clutching her side where she had also been struck by a bullet.

A group of four sailors dropped to their deck and began shouting at them to lay on their stomachs with their hands behind their heads. Citrine set Pearl calmly down beside the main mast, drew out his knife and hurled it into the chest of the closest sailor.

The fight began in earnest. Bullets and knives flew through the air; it was impossible to tell what belonged to whom, or who the intended target was. Mira shot down one man with her pistol and tore her dagger through another man's belly, he let out a scream and she tore it out and drove it up into the bottom of his chin.

Topaz was battling short swords with another man, and stopped as Mira dropped to one knee, exhausted. The man took the advantage of his distraction and sliced through Topaz's forearm. He let out a cry of pain and jumped back, holding his arm to his chest. Mira threw another dagger at the man and it stuck into his shoulder, when he turned around to face her, Topaz drove his short sword home into his back. They shared a quick nod and turned to fight the next man.

They were quickly losing handle of the situation, more men were dropping from the other ship and even more were firing from its deck. Mira watched as Spinel dragged Tanzanite away from the dead man and dropped him over the side of the ship yelling at him to swim to shore. Peridot was hovering over Pearl's unconscious body, holding her penknife with both hands thrusting it at anyone who came near. Elizabeth was still nowhere to be seen.

"Dar she blows! Abandon ship!" Mira whirled, looking skyward. Why did that blasted bird have to stay on the ship?

Movement caught her eye, Emerald crawled over the side of the ship, keeping low and headed toward Peridot and Pearl. Mira let out a war cry as she saw a man ran after the girl.

"Get out of here!" Mira shouted at the girl, "I told you to get away from here!" She shot at the man as he grew closer to Emerald and missed, she flung her dagger and it flew too wide. In an act of desperation, she ran at him and flung herself onto his back, wrapped her good arm around his throat and squeezed with all of her might. The man tried shaking her off, but stumbled.

"Get off you flea!" He hollered, swatting at her hands.

Topaz came out of nowhere and struck the man in the stomach. "They've taken her!" He yelled to Mira. "They took Elizabeth. We must go, now!"

Mira looked to the other ship; sure enough she could see Elizabeth, her hands tied behind her back, being held by what must be the captain. She struggled against the man as he wrenched open the front of her dress, displaying her bare chest. She turned wildly back to the Oddity's Revenge, when she spotted Mira running toward her, she screamed, "Kill me!"

"No!" Mira screamed in return. She tried to catch a rope that was attached to the other ship but arms encircled her waist and she was slammed into the deck.

A sailor was on top of her, blood dripping from a cut on his forehead. His knees pinned her shoulders and his hands wrapped around her throat. She grunted against the pain in her shoulder and kicked out, trying to buck him off. Her vision was going blurry and she could feel herself slipping away, he squeezed harder, and she closed her eyes. She could feel his blood dripping onto her face, but she didn't care.

Her friends' eyes flashed behind her lids. Topaz's a muddy green, the first time their eyes met. Peridot's a piercing blue, when she lifted her veil to reveal her red-rimmed eyes. Spinel's a soft amber, full of wonder at the sight of her ship. The twins' a pale blue, pleading with her to let them leave with her. Emerald's dark brown, and full of mischief. And Elizabeth's cerulean, full of suspicion, lust, and ready for anything. She had lived a good life, hadn't she? She had adventure, joy, and love. She had her fill of heartbreak, disappointment and agony.

Her thoughts lingered on Topaz and Elizabeth; she smiled, welcoming the darkness as her blood ran cold.

She suddenly felt the hands leave her neck. The warmness seeped back into her body, and she gasped. Her eyes flew open and there was Topaz, holding her face and saying something she couldn't make out, she realized slowly that she could only hear a loud ringing sound.

"What?" She gasped.

"I said Citrine saw Elizabeth jump into the sea. Emerald came after us in a rowboat, the clever little thing. We must go Mira, now!" He picked her up and carried her as best he could to the far side of the boat. She looked down to see Pearl, Emerald and Peridot in a tiny rowboat that surely wasn't big enough for them all, Citrine was climbing down the rope after them.

"Look!" Emerald yelled, pointing toward the aft of the ship. "It's Miss Zircon!"

Sure enough, Elizabeth was swimming toward them, panting heavily as her heavy dress dragged her down.

"Please don't leave me! Kill me if you must, but don't let them take me!" She yelled as best she could.

Spinel dived into the water nearby and started swimming for shore, Mira would bet her life to say that she was going after Tanzanite.

"Down the ladder, Love. Slowly now, we can't have you in worse shape than you already are," Topaz told her.

She started down the ladder and looked up to meet his eyes, her ears still ringing, when he made a very funny face. She let out a small laugh and said, "What are you making that face for?"

But he didn't answer her, he leaned forward as if to give her a kiss, and fell. Mira gave a cry of alarm and reached out to catch his forearm, the one that had been sliced open only moments before.

He screamed in pain as the wound opened and blood flowed down his arm. She followed the trail of blood to see his shirt ripped open and realization struck her. He had been shot through the chest. She let out a blood-curdling scream and clutched him tighter.

"No, not yet! Do you hear me? Not yet!" She screamed.

She looked back over the deck of the ship, swearing that she would kill the man that did this to him. Standing on the railing of the opposite ship was a familiar face, smiling the black smile that haunted her dreams. Her eyes widened in horror and fury as he dragged a thumb across his neck at her.

"Thomas." She whispered. She hadn't seen the First Mate in twelve years.

"Mira," Topaz rasped. Her attention was torn back to him, and saw that he was tucking his good hand into his breeches pocket. The look in his eyes tore Mira in two.

"Take care of them, my love. Forgive yourself and let the past lie. Save them all, the crew and everyone else that needs you. And for the love of the sea Mira, love her. Love her like you never allowed yourself to love me. I will be with you always, Mira." He touched her lips with his free hand, placed something in her hand and then let go, never breaking eye contact until his body slammed into the water below.

Mira stared in horror, then let go of the ladder, determined to follow him to the bottom of the sea. She hit the water and tried to plunge deeper but a too gentle hand caught her ankle and pulled her up. When her head broke free, she screamed, she didn't stop screaming when Citrine pulled her into the small craft and began rowing them away. She screamed as she turned back and realized that they had set fire to her beloved ship; or when they had reached shore and ran for their lives into the hills of the village beyond. Those same gentle hands pulled her along as she screamed and grieved. She grieved for the loss of her two greatest loves, and for the life that she had lived with them.

In her mind, she never stopped screaming.

Epilogue
Two years later

Mira Tourmaline lives on a quiet piece of property high, in a small leaky barn on a cliff overlooking the sea. She lives with a peculiar group of people, some of the near by villagers called them odd when they first arrived, but none have made the mistake since. She had knocked a few teeth out of the man who had muttered the word at them, and wore them in her hair the next time she came to town.

Her beard, once well kept and short, has grown to a considerable length and she is often asked to trim it, but she refuses. She still wears a sailor's outfit, breeches, a loose fitting shirt and soft leather boots. She lost her beloved top hat and goggles a long time ago. She also wears an enormous diamond ring on the middle finger of her left hand, which she has never taken off sine it was placed there two years ago.

She spends her days sitting in the sun, looking out over the ocean, dreaming of a life she used to live. The others she lives with often dream of similar things, but not as much as she does, they have accepted their fates and have learned to love the land.

All accept one, who trails close behind her as she walks along the cliffs. She is her shadow by day and her savior by night, lying in bed with her arms draped tightly around her shoulders, and hushing her as she cries.

In the evenings she sits on the front porch, smoking a pipe and waiting for a young girl to appear with news. This girl is gone for days, sometimes months at a time, but she always returns bringing stories of her travels, but not much news.

Tonight is different. Mira sees the girl walking up the long dirt road to the small leaky house, and she doesn't drop her bag.

"I have news, Miss Mira." The girl says.

"Someone needs your help."

Mira nods, her shadow stiffens.

"Very well," she says, the first words she's spoken in years.